BONGO FURY

NOVELLA COLLECTION

& MINI ALBUM

STONE OF THE HOUND
PUBLISHING

Also by Simon Maltman

A Chaser on the Rocks

A Kill for the Poet

The Sidewinder

More Faces: Short Story Collection

STONE OF THE
HOUND
PUBLISHING

Bongo Fury: Novella Collection

Simon Maltman

This is a work of fiction. Names, characters, businesses, places, events and incidents are either the products of the author's imagination or used in a fictitious manner. Any resemblance to actual persons, living or dead, or actual events is purely coincidental.

Copyright Simon Maltman 2019

First published 2019

STONE OF THE HOUND
PUBLISHING

Dedicated to the long gone record stores
from my youth.

Index

Download your free accompanying mini album here:
https://bit.ly/2JzPMFN

...

Bongo Fury
Novella Collection
Mini Album

By

Simon Maltman

1. In Absentia

2. Waiting Outside

3. Head Over Heart

4. Fault Line

5. Creeping Back Home

(all songs written and performed by

Simon Maltman

C. 2019)

Bongo Fury

Chapter 1

So, first thing's first; I didn't expect things to get as fucked up as they did. But it happens, so that's life I suppose. I just don't want people getting the wrong impression about me. I'm not just some hard-nut wanker who came out of the estates. Yeah, I'm a Prod, from an estate in Northern Ireland- but that doesn't define me. I've got a fucking literature degree- I've read Mansfield Park- okay? I actually quite liked it too. Anyway, I suppose I'd better go back to the start.

Two years ago, life was pretty normal. If you're reading this, then I suppose you already know I'm Jimmy Black, I'm forty two and I come from Ards in Northern Ireland. You're bound to have read about me in the tabloids. I'm the one covered in tats, pretty well built, short black hair, and I admit not the prettiest you'll see in the papers. If you've never heard of Ards before then that's because it's a shithole. However, it does have a lovely old tower on the hill called Scrabo; from where you can survey the shithole.

Anyway, I live there- or did, and I worked in Bangor- the town up the road. Now, Bangorians are different from the inbreds in Ards. They think they're fucking living In Monaco or something. You'd expect to scc Grace Kelly resident at the Town Hall. I digress. So, I had a shop in Bangor called Bongo Fury. Yeah it's a pretty cool name. It was a nice little music shop with musical equipment, and a vinyl section too. Any of you music aficionados out there will realise the namesake was an album by Captain Beefheart and Frank Zappa. It's a great live album that provided me with a tenuous link for my musical instrument shop. Well there you have it. It didn't do a great trade, but I really did love that shop. It was also the only place around to get strings or records that wasn't on-fucking-line. So many good music shops went bust the last lot of years. Loads in Bangor had all closed, until there were none- but not just Bangor. Belfast had only one or two left. Like Good Vibrations- opening and reopening over and over again! They even made a movie about the owner Teri Hooley, and he still can't keep its doors open today. Maybe one day there'll be a movie about me too. So, I ran it myself, and on this particular day- it was a Tuesday I think- I had had shite all customers in so far. I was enjoying a cuppa, a biscuit, and just chilling out. It was about 11am and in walks Big Stevie. Now, Stevie and me went way back, from knocking about together when we were kids on the estate. We both were in trouble a good bit back then, but I had wised up by the time I was out of my teens. Stevie hadn't. I never got that involved with the paramilitaries, despite my family tree being like a who's who of Loyalist crims. Stevie dipped in and out of it and at this point he was mostly out.

"What about you Stevie?" I said, as he ambled into the shop. His long, greasy hair swayed over his blue denim jacket. He was actually double-deniming it that day; blue jeans finishing the ensemble. Never was the most stylish man.

"Alright Jim, ya ball beg," said Stevie, in his usually colourful way.

He walked past the guitars and stood at the other side of the counter, and we had a wee chat. He almost knocked into a lovely second hand Les Paul, the big eejit.

"Watch my new sunburst Stevie," I said, "If you're gonna bang into something- make it a Stagg."

I put the kettle on and we had a brew together over the counter. The shop wasn't very big. I had about a dozen guitars, a couple of keyboards, and a few other instruments.

Mostly, I had lots of general bollox- like strings, plectrums and drum skins. There were lots of posters on the walls and shit, and really the place looked a pretty decent job. Of course I also had a bongo- but that was just for the window display. It was a little ways out of the town centre, up towards the Abbey; but the passing trade wasn't bad. I had some decent regulars too, who were good craic.

"How's the wee one doing?" he asked, taking a slug of his second cup. I told him she was fine. That's my daughter- Skye-she was about one at the time. My wee sweetheart.

"How about your crew?" I asked him.

"They're wee shites!" he said, making a face. I laughed. Stevie was good craic- he wasn't a hood as such. He just was good at making bad decisions sometimes.

"Look, the reason I called in, is to ask a favour," said Stevie, giving me his pleading side smile. I'd seen it a brave lot over the years.

"Go on- I didn't think it was close enough to the twelfth for you to need a new snare skin. What are you after?"

"Well, not so much a favour- more of a wee job if you're up for it. You know- the kind of thing you've done before."

That was one way I supplemented my income a bit. I had a wee sideline. Maybe it was more of a fault line. Somehow I fell into being the go to guy for sorting out a variety of problems. I'm not a fucking PI, but I help people out and they pay me for it. No, I never declared it for my taxes- not that it matters much now. Yes, I got paid- I'm not bloody Oxfam. My place in the community, because of my family, gave me some standing and I've always been well built and suppose given off a certain confidence. I'm really not that cocky and I tend to finish fights- not start them, but people seemed to always trust me and think I'll look after them. Because I wasn't actually involved in any particular faction and was merely 'connected,' that also seemed to help people come to me as well. Anyway, I'd try and sort shit out for people if I thought I could, and they'd usually bung me a few quid for it. I was like Philip Marlowe on Buckfast to the local prods. Not that I wouldn't have helped out a Catholic- I've no time for all that sectarian shite- but most would probably sooner swear allegiance to her majesty, than come to me.

"Ok, go on," I said to him.

He frowned, "It's just I know you're mates with Davy Dick and…"

"Well, not really mates," I interrupted.

Davy Dick was the owner of Dawson's pool room and I would drink there from time to time. He was really called Davy Dawson, but everyone referred to him as Davy Dick... because he was a bit of a dick.

"Well, I know you talked to him for Glenn a few years back and I was..."

"You owe him some money and you want me to get him off your back?" I said, interrupting again.

Stevie blew out some air and gave me a shrug,

"Well, yeah. If you would, like... I'd appreciate it Jim. You'd be helpin' me out big style."

He looked anxious, then shot me another thin smile- displaying his crooked and yellowing teeth.
He glanced at the door and then lowered his voice a little. He didn't need to worry as it was two hours until I had another customer- nobody else came in the whole time we were chatting. My next patron was a wee tit who called in later on and wanted a Snow Patrol chord book. Fucking Snow Patrol! I told him I didn't have one and instead talked him into buying Troublegum by Therapy? on green vinyl. Twat.

"I owe him nearly a grand Jim, and I just don't have anywhere near it. I'm waitin' on a few wee deals coming through and then I should be sweet. But I can't pay him it all at once."

"Look Stevie, I won't make you any promises," I said, feeling sorry for the guy. He was my mate, even if he was a div, "I'll talk to him- but that's all. You know he's got guys standing over him and I'm not going to be giving him a hard time. I can't go to war with him."

"No, no- mate, that would be fuckin' A," he said and I swear a bit of colour returned to his cheeks, "You're a legend," he added.

We had another brew, and then Stevie headed out with promises that he would sort me out when he was flush again, and he'd do this for me, and that for me. He was a mate and I didn't care if I got any money from him or not. I didn't count on all the shit I'd get over it either.

Chapter 2

I closed up for the day at about half three, as I hadn't even sold fifty quid's worth of stuff, and I was a bit pissed off. I got into my seven year old silver Audi, and fired straight on up the road to the pool hall. It was off the ring road, on my way home to Ards. The sun was high in the sky overhead. I whistled along to 'Us and them' by The Floyd, as I went- feeling better being out of the shop and enjoying the cool air whistling back at me through the cracked open window. Dawson's was an old working man's club, popular with paramilitary Union lovers, and pool lovers alike. The outside had been white once upon a time, but much of it was bereft even of render. There was a faded green tinge to the walls inside, and it was the only bar you could still smoke in where no one would say anything to you- police included. When you stepped inside, you were stepping back into the 1980's; both in décor and attitudes.

"Pint of Smithwicks please Julie," I said, inadvertently licking my lips.

"Do you want a shandy top on it tonight Jimmy?"

"No cheers love, I'm feeling dangerous."

Julie was a good looking brunette, in her late twenties. She had been working in the bar for about a year and I have to say having her around brightened the place up. Not that I went there very often- it was a bit rough even for me. Her predecessor- girl by the name of Jen Bradley had tried ripping off the place the year before. Apparently she lost a few fingers for her trouble and went off to live in England.

"Jimmy," said Davy, resting a heavy palm on my arm. His voice was hoarse as usual and his stale tobacco breath; worse than most horses'.

"What about you David?" I said cracking a smile, and taking his hand and shaking it.

Davy Dick was mid fifties, with short greying hair and two pencil prick eyes. He was in a brown suit; a little old fashioned, even for that bar.

"Knocking off early today then?" he said, leaning against the bar, his moustache dancing on his upper lip as he spoke.

"Yeah it was shite today pal. Thought I'd play a few frames before heading home and the whole: making the baby's bottles, and putting her to bed and all that."

"Jimmy Black- the modern father personified! Never though I'd see the day," he said, with an even smile. He still looked a smarmy get.

"Well, you've got to do your bit," I added, stopping to take a swig, "Quick game?" I asked, raising my half empty glass.

"Yeah, rack 'em up," he said, pulling off his jackct.

We played two games and won one each. I waited till the third one to bring it up.

"Look Davy, I actually needed to talk to you about something, while I'm here."

"I wondered why you let me win that second game, g'wan ahead," he said, focusing on chalking up his cue.

"It's about Big Stevie."

"That wee prick? For fucksake."

He looked over at me, mildly frustrated, and then fingered out a cigarette from a fake black leather case.

"You want one?" he asked, his tone less amicable.

"Nah, cheers Davy, trying to stay off 'em."

He blew out a small cloud of smoke and gestured with his cigarette,

"Look Jimmy, I lent him money on good faith. On good faith a couple of times actually, and again even a bit when the faith was dried up. He's got to pay me back sometime for fucksake, and he's had plenty of chances."

He sounded reasonable enough about it, I supposed. He bent down, took a shot, and missed- pocketing the white while he was at it. I could tell then that he was trying hard not to lose his shit.

"I know what he's like. He's a twat at times Dave, but he's a good lad really. I'm just askin' for a wee bit more time for him. He's waiting on some money coming in he says." I tried to sound casual and breezy, which is hard enough when you look like me.

I chalked up my own cue, blew off the dust, and then pocketed two yellows- missing a third on the middle pocket. He shook his head in a non-committal kind of way and took his shot carefully, pocketing one of his reds in the top corner. He leaned over the table and considered the white, looking to pot an awkward ball off the bottom cushion. He straightened up and gave me a hard stare.

"Two weeks. Then that's it. And only as a favour to you. You owe me one."

"I appreciate it. I'll see that you get paid," I said.

He stubbed out his cigarette carefully in an ashtray on the table, then chalked his cue again, "I know you will, it's not just me he owes though Jim."

He leaned back down to take his shot, and missed.

Chapter 3

Davy Dick didn't say anything more than that, and I was happy enough I had bought Stevie some more time. I'd tried to sound reasonable, speak plainly- head over heart. I finished my second pint and then drove on home. I lived on the side of Ards out towards Comber- the nicer side if you will. It's a bit like saying one side's nicer after taking a shite. No, it's actually okay- and Comber's a nice spot. Bit snobby maybe. I'm not one for watching my P's and Q's, like some of those *hoity toity* pricks who lived near me. Our house was a tidy wee end of terrace, a good enough street; certainly a million miles from the estates I've lived on. It was about six when I got home, and Pavla and Skye were in the kitchen.

"You're late," said Pavla, with a mildly cross look on her face.

"I'm sorry love," I said, making a beeline for Skye on her playmate.

"Da-doo," said Skye.

Close enough, I thought. I picked her up and gave her a cuddle.

"Hows my angel?"

She didn't reply because she could say fuck all yet. I carried her back to her playmate and lay down beside her, helping her build some blocks.

"Well, how have you been love?" I called over to Pavla, as she irately stirred a pot on the hob.
Pavla and me had been together about four years by then. She's from Poland and we met at a bar in Ards. Well, it was really in the Chinese beside where we got some munch in after a night's wreckin'. Davy Lees- it was famous in Ards. I think I had a curry half and half. Anyway, we just clicked and it wasn't too long until we were living together, and then Skye came along too.

"Okay Jimmy, but a text or call would 'been nice," she answered, straining some veg over the sink.
I stood up, gave Skye a kiss and walked over to Pavla. I turned off Steve Wright coming from the radio beside her, and gave her a cheeky pinch on the bum. She slapped my hand away.

"Aww fuck up or I'll send you back to work in the carwash," I teased, grabbing her around the waist and kissing her. She smirked and then turned back to her cooking.

"Next time just give me a fucking text, now go and set 'table," she said, fortunately in a playful tone.

We had a delish meal; Pavla can fucking cook. I gave Skye her bottle after and put her down. I remember it was an all round good evening. We watched some T.V, then while Pavla popped out to Tesco, I read a bit of my new John Coltrane biography. Fucking nuts- the guy was on smack, got clean, then became an alco, got clean again, then in the Sixties he got into acid and ate so many sweets that most of his teeth fell out. But could he ever play? I'm not a total jazz-head, but sometimes it's just the ticket. Anyway, when she got back from the shops, we took a bottle of wine up to the bedroom and watched a film on the laptop- bliss!

Chapter 4

I woke up the next morning with a throbbing head. Just a small one- not like after a proper *sesh*. Pavla had got up half an hour before me and was giving Skye her bottle in the baby room. I pulled myself out of bed and straightened out my back. I put on my slippers (because I'm an old fucker now) and navigated my way downstairs. The kettle was boiled, and I was just putting ground coffee into the cafetiere, when my mobile went off. My ringtone was Prince- Dirty Mind. It doesn't matter who's calling when that's on- always makes me feel like boogying. It was a landline number that I didn't recognise.

"Hello."

Silence, then a crackling.

"Hello?" I said again.

There was a muffled noise- like the receiver being pulled over something, and I'd swear I heard my name called. A click, then silence. Setting the phone down, I poured the boiling water up to the top of the percolator- enough for two cups each for Pav and me. I thought about who might be calling.

It felt a bit funny. I waited for them to ring again while the coffee brewed. It didn't. By the time I had buttered our toast, I had forgotten about it. Pavla brought Skye down and I played with her in her highchair, while drinking my coffee. I kissed them goodbye and headed into work for around 9am.

Chapter 5

I always tried to get in for 9am, even though it could be almost afternoon before any fucker darkened my shop door. I had the shutter up and another cup of coffee in my hand by half past. I read a bit of Classic Rock magazine and played about on Facebook. I sent Pavla a couple of texts. To my surprise, I actually had a few customers early on. They all spent less than a tenner, but cash is cash. The morning was uneventful and I closed up for an hour at lunch and went round to 'The Diner' café'. They did an amazing Ulster fry and chips. Two fucking plates full! Anyway, when I got back to the shop, I found the door ajar and the shitty lock had been broken off. I couldn't see anyone inside, as I eased in around the door, my fists ready. Two men then casually sauntered out from my back room.

"Hello Jimmy," leered the first one. He was around my age, thinning on top, a thin face and a thin smile. The second was about twenty, still a little puffy faced and puffed up with youth. He had an earring, but enough muscle to avoid being called a fruit.

"Who the fuck are you two clowns?" I demanded, getting ready for a scuffle. I wasn't as fit as a butcher's dog like I'd used to be, but I was still tight enough.

"Less of the cheek," said Thin, "Sit the fuck down."

"Go fuck yourself," I said, moving closer. Puff shuffled a little on the spot.

"We're here to talk to you Jim- that's all," said Thin.

"Well, you didn't need to break my friggen front door then, did you? What d'ya want?"

"Will we go in the back and talk Jim?" said Thin, gesturing benevolently with his hand.

They both moved to the side of the counter to let me pass.

"Sure," I said.

I took two quick steps and my right fist made mashed spuds of Puff's nose. He fell backwards, trying to suppress the spray of blood with both hands. He let out a muffled

'Fuuuuuck!'

Thin reached swiftly into his left breast pocket, but I punched him hard in the arm, damn near breaking bone.

He gave a little yelp, like a Rottweiler stubbing its toe. I gave him a hard two jabs to his right cheek. He went down too. It wasn't that hard. I've still got the bulk. They were both stunned and I casually collected a pistol from each of them.

I checked them over. Puff's wasn't even loaded. Throwing the guns behind me, I stood over my two assailants and waited patiently to listen to the inevitable threats.

"You're fucking dead now Black. You shouldn't have done this," said Thin, getting to his knees and trying to regain some composure.

"Really?" I said, lifting a small children's pink ukulele off the wall, "Try a different tune."

I smashed it off his head and it made a satisfying crunch. It only dazed him a little, it was more for the craic. Puff was on his honkers too, trying to look tough again, but failing miserably. I pointed at him.

"It'll be a fucking double-bass on your loaf if you give me any trouble," I said.

He looked down at the floor, seething.

Thin had lost a fair proportion of his machismo and clearly wasn't used to being treated like this- but I didn't give two fucks.

"Bestie sent us," said Thin quietly, through his teeth. Now that took a little of the wind out of me.

"Bestie Nine-mill?" I asked, trying not to sound phased.

"Yeah," he said, pleased with himself.

"What the fuck for?" I said, giving his a hard look.

"We're to warn you off putting your nose into things that don't concern you- like that friend of yours Stevie." He started to brush back his hair with a small black comb and gather himself. Puff continued to look at the floor.

"What the fuck has that got to do with him? Fucksake fellas," I said, shrugging with both my hands I hovered for a second, a little off centre. 'Shite!' I thought. I helped them both up to their feet. Fucksake- I felt like a right lapper. But a wise man has to play the politician sometimes. Just look at Northern Ireland.

"No hard feelings huh?" I said, "I can't be having people breaking into my place and giving me shit, you know? But I mean no disrespect to Bestie."
They straightened themselves up some more, as best they could. It was hard; they were both bleeding and pink bits of ukulele were lying all round the gaff. To be fair; they looked a fucking state. I tried not to laugh.

"Go fuck yourself," said Thin coldly, and they both left. He emphasised the 'your.'

I picked up the remains of the ukulele off the floor and held it absently in my hand, staring out the window. Two school kids ambled past the glass. They looked in at me and stopped.

"Fucking big fairy," shouted one, both then ran off. I didn't respond, because I was trying to work out what one of the biggest local hoods wanted with me and Stevie.

Chapter 6

The afternoon dragged in. I was in a bit of disbelief and was more than a little worried about what I had gotten myself into. I fixed up the lock on my door as best I could, more as a distraction than anything else. Why the hell was Nine-mill involved? It didn't make much sense. I had a girl and a kid now and I couldn't go running around not caring who I pissed off as much I used to. He certainly wasn't someone to go pissing off. Besides, I was in my forties now and I suppose I was getting a little more sensible. In saying that, the more I sat in my empty shop thinking things through, the angrier I got. I hadn't done anything to anyone and my shop gets broke into and two clampets start on me. What was bloody Davy playing at-after saying all was fine? I wasn't having it! I shut up a few hours early, with my heart beating out of my chest, and drove straight over to Davy Dick's place. My temper didn't ease as I drove. When I jumped out, I left sweaty stains behind on the steering wheel.

Chapter 7

I punched him hard in the stomach, instantly winding him. He doubled over and gagged.

"We're all out of cheese and onion crisps you prick," I said, pushing him back into the little room.

I had sat around the side of the club for about twenty minutes, and smoked a roll up to calm my nerves. Davy wasn't a massive player by local standards, but he'd usually have a few crim mates hanging around at any given time in the bar. I thought I'd like to avoid any additional trouble. I had walked around the back of the building, where there was only a bit of wasteland and some extra parking spaces that were never needed. I found the window for Davy's office and had peered in. I could make him out at the far right of his room, sitting at his desk; smoking, and typing on his computer. There was a fire door on round from where I was standing. It wasn't far from where the shutters were at the other side of the back wall, where all the kegs and shit get loaded in. I had walked up to the door and hammered on it.

"Tayto delivery," I had shouted gruffly at the door.

He had answered after a second or two. I pushed him onto the floor and blocked his exit to the bar, putting myself between him and any heavies who might come in. A few minutes later and he still hadn't got his breath back. Luckily no one else came running. I towered over him and gave him my best pissed off grimace. I didn't really have to try.

"You really are such a dick, Davy Dick," I spat.
He shot me a glare from the floor, as he loosened his tie, breathing heavily.

"What's the story- why did you set Nine-mill on me?" I hissed.

He composed himself better, and his breathing sounded like he only smoked fifty a day.

"I don't know what you're on about you fucking nut job!" he rasped.

I shook my head with a mocking smile.

"Ahhh!" he cried, as I gave him a hard boot in the spine.

"Okay! Alright," he said, and sat up, wiping hair out of his eyes.

He was clearly fucking annoyed at being in this position; when he was used to swaggering about like Robert De Niro. He wasn't even Café' Nero.

"It's your own fucking fault Jim. I told you that Stevie owed all over town."

"Yeah, but why does that mean two fucking twats come and break into my shop?"

"Look, I had to mention you to Nine-mill. I didn't want him to go after you, really Jim. But I suppose he wanted to warn you off interfering."

"You fucking rat. You're full of shit- do you know that? It suited you to get Nine-mill onto Stevie, 'cause maybe you'd get your money sooner then too. Shake him hard enough and a few pennies might drop out your way."

"I didn't go looking for any shite you know? Get the fuck out of my bar- you're lucky if I don't get you knee capped for this."

He went to stand up. I grabbed him by the tie and tightened it around his neck.

"Don't you ever threaten me you fuck! We go back Davy you and I, and I know a thing or three about you. You're a 'Del boy' and nothing more. You give me anymore shit and I'll get the really big boys onto you."

I let him go and he slumped down onto the floor, gasping even more than earlier. I regarded him with disgust and shook my head. I was fucking furious at how this was all playing out.

I glared at him some more, I could feel my eyes blazing. Striding over to his computer, I picked it up and smashed it onto the floor, before leaving again through the fire escape. I didn't turn around to see what his face looked like.

Chapter 8

That night was shitty. It was a weird one. I didn't know if I was coming or going. It reminded me of when I was at university and tripping off my tits. Everything was squiffy. I had arrived home in a bit of a daze and helped with Skye's putdown. I had a spot of dinner and Pav talked about her NVQ3, and I went through the motions with it all. I was really zoned out and thinking of knee cappings and ukulele smashings. Pavla went into the living room to do some study and I told her I was going up to the attic for a while, and would be down in a bit. My attic was a decent conversion job. I had a carpet down and a couple of old sofas. There were a few vinyls on the wall and I had a pretty good stereo set up in there. You'd maybe call it a 'Man Cave' these days. The only downside was trying to get my forty-odd old self up and down the rickety ladder. I tried ringing Stevie, but it just went straight to voicemail. I sat down and a put some John Coltrane on. After about five minutes my heart was racing through a mix of anxiety and probably the free jazz wasn't helping any. I switched to some Bill Evans trio and sparked up a spliff. I wasn't a big toker, more a drinker, but I liked a couple of nights on it in the week. Pavla knew I smoked a bit, but she didn't know about the rest. That was the other wee bit of my income. I did a bit of growing in my attic. Nothing major; just a few plants, and I won't mention how many due to any upcoming legal wrangles! Anyway, it was a nice wee sideline and quite profitable too. It did better than my fucking shop did- which was also a handy place to sell some out of. Anyway. I tried to get into the music and enjoy the smoke, but I was still on edge. I didn't know what my next move should be. Maybe I had over reacted. My stomach turned stale and I put the smoke out. I felt panicky. I couldn't let my family be in any danger. I hadn't been in serious trouble in ages. Maybe I had let my temper get the better of me. No- fuck this! I clenched my fists. I had had a wobble, but I wasn't going to be intimidated by those pricks. I changed record to early Chilli Peppers, rolled a new joint and formulated my plan of attack.

…

I enjoyed a nice breakfast the next morning. Pavla had made me bacon and soda, and Skye was in good form before nursery. I had decided roughly on what I was gonna do and I knew I needed to get some help. I was in work for the usual time and was feeling better. I had a few cups of filter coffee and enjoyed chatting to a couple of actual real live customers. I only glanced towards the door nervously a few times. I tried ringing Stevie again, but it just came through as unable to connect the call. Lunchtime came and went and my chum Brian called in. Brian was a guy I had known since Uni and was about my only friend who didn't adorn his house with flags and coloured hands. He was older than me though and did a bit of everything- including a bit of light dealing on the side. Didn't touch the stuff himself. He actually used to be a cop. I gave him a few bags every couple of days and we had a nice wee set up going. I had a few guys like Brian, who would call in through the week and that's how I preferred to run that side of things. It certainly beats guys turning up at your door, waiting outside strung out and wanting a bag of grass.

"Any sign of those new reissues?" Brian asked, leafing through some of my vinyls. We had finished our other transaction and he was having a look round the shop.

"Was it the new Soundgarden one you wanted?"

"No- Temple of the Dog."

"Oh yeah, that's right- think there's one copy there."
He had a leaf through and found it, plucking it out with a wide grin,

"Beezer," he said, bringing it up to the counter.

"Fifteen ninety-nine," I said, reading the label, "Call it an even fifteen."

"You're too kind Jim," he said.

The call came towards the end of the day and I was surprised they had left it that late. I suppose they wanted me to sweat. The phone rang about fourish.

"Hello, Bongo Fury, Jim speaking."

"You're to come for a meeting Jimmy."

I didn't recognise the voice.

"With who?"

"Four thirty at number 11, Dury Drive. Don't keep us waiting."

"Who's this?"

The line went flat and I put down the phone. Chewing my lip, I lifted my rucksack up that I had stuffed under the counter. I double checked my snub nose was loaded.

Chapter 9

I took a piss before shutting up shop and going out to the car. I drank a bottle of Corona as I drove, just to take the edge off. One day I'd do a full day's work, I thought to myself, shaking my head. It was warm and I could feel sweat dripping from my pits underneath my short-sleeved shirt. I swung into the estate and parked up outside my brother's mid terrace. I hadn't seen Leo in about six months- the last time we had ended up fighting after watching a Linfield/ Celtic friendly. We wouldn't have been the only ones fighting that night.

"What d'ya want?"

That was the friendly greeting I received, as the door was answered. It was Leo's wife Tracy. Leo's a few years older than me, but more than double her age. She's an attractive enough girl, but the 'smacked arse' face kind of ruins it.

"Nice to see you too, is he in?" I asked, flashing a sarcastic grin. We had never got on.

"Maybe he is, but…"

"Who is it?" came a holler from behind her. She tutted, then carried on chewing hard on her bubblegum.

"Fucksake it's you," said Leo, appearing at her side, with a half smile. Tracy chomped hard on her lip, then stomped off.

"It's me, so like can I come in?" I said.

"C'mon in, can't have you making the place look shabby," he said, almost warmly.

We walked down the hall, avoiding children's scooters and bikes, as he led me into the living room. The snooker was on and a fresh can of Harp was leaving little bubbles of perspiration on the glass table.

"You want one?" he said following my gaze, lighting up a fag.

"Aye go on, cheers."

Once we had a drink in hand, we sat down and Leo switched off the telly. It was a cosy enough wee room- bit messy and the pair of them had bloody god-awful taste, but who am I?

"So, it's been a while Jimmy," he said, sipping from the can. He was wearing a black shirt and jeans, sporting the usual closely cropped hair. There were a few patches starting to show where the light hit his head right. He had always been a thinner man than me and still was, though there was a small paunch now at the front; mostly full of Harp.

"I'm sorry about that Leo, you know- we've been busy. We must all meet up- get Pav and Skye round or whatever. See your clan too."

"Aye sure," he said sulkily.

"Come on Leo, you know how it goes?"

"Aye, I know you think you're too good for us now," he said, wiping his mouth on his sleeve.

"Don't be fucking daft," I said, irritably, "I don't think anything, we've just been busy, so, how are you anyway?" I said, hoping to keep things civil.

"I'm alright. She's alright," he said without much enthusiasm, "kids are at school, they're fucking nuts."

"I've all that ahead," I said and smirked.

"Aye you do," said Leo, warming up and even letting out a chuckle.

There was a brief silence, as we slugged our tinnies. It reminded me of when we were kids. He sat back, then crushed up his can and threw it in a wicker bin beside him.

"Fucksake Jim, get to the point would you?" he said, half joking, "You obviously want something?"
I made a face. Then I told him about Big Stevie, Davy Dick and Bestie Nine-mill.

"Jesus wept," he said, shaking his head, "you've a way of getting into these scrapes, haven't you?"

"It seems that way," I said shrugging, "I don't fuckin' know how. I was just trying to look out for a mate."
Leo put his second can down and lit up a smoke, rolling his eyes.

"Shit- fuckin' Nine-mill, not good Jimmy. I suppose you're wanting big brother to sort everything out for ya?"

"Look, I thought maybe you could put a wee word in- you're higher up than Davy Dick- right?"

"Yeah, course, but I'm nowhere near Nine-mill. He might talk to me- but he's not gonna listen to much I have to say."

"Well I don't much wanna lose a finger or one of my knees, so I thought I'd see if you can help me."

"What time you meeting them?" he said scratching his neck and looking away.

I checked my watch, "About an hour."

"Bloody Nora. G'wan then, I'll come with ya."

"Listen Leo, I appreciate it, I'll owe you one."

"Yeah you will," he said, downing the rest of his can.

He leaned back and blew out his cheeks.

He turned on the snooker again and we watched a frame.

"Are you packin'?" he asked suddenly.

"Yeah."

"Leave it in the car. They search us on the way in and find guns, Nine-mill would go fucking berserk."

Chapter 10

I drove the Audi and we both smoked as we made the short trip. It was just after ten to, when we got there. It was another unassuming terrace in a nearby estate; Leo said it was a house used for various business meetings and indeed business beatings.

"Look Leo, I thought I'd pretty much be straight up with him; tell him how I just asked Davy to ease up and he agreed. Then next thing I know he had gone up the chain and was putting heat on me. What do you think?"

"I dunno Jim, it depends what mood he's in. Moody fucker is Nine-mill. Start off that way I suppose and then I'll see if I can find an angle. It'll be alright. Safe as milk. Just don't lose that fucking temper of yours."

…

"Big brother here to hold your dick?" said Thin, answering the door.

"He's here in case you try and grab it first," I replied,

"Now are you gonna fucking let us in or what?"

Leo grabbed my elbow to say to keep calm.

Thin switched on a fake smile, and bowed theatrically at my brother. Leo frowned.

"First gentlemen, formalities I'm afraid," said Thin, moving forward and patting us down. He patted me first, then Leo. He grinned as he did so.

"Don't enjoy it too much," said Leo, expressionless. Thin looked bored now.

"Right, come on through then," he said.

He led us past a small sitting room, where a couple of goons were drinking and playing cards. We then came into the kitchen where a nice extension had been built onto the back, with double doors leading out to the garden. Thin gestured disinterestedly, indicating for us to take a seat. There was nobody in the room, but somebody was outside smoking- their back against the glass doors. The greying ponytail was a giveaway; it was Nine-mill. We sat there for a moment and Thin went and stood by the door we had come through. Nine-mill threw down his cig, stomped it out and turned around. Before he came in, the wrinkled face of a hard living man entering his fifties fixed me a stare. The still bright green eyes were deep set and thatched by two bushy eyebrows.

"Thanks for coming," he called coldly to me, as he entered the room, "Leo, I wasn't expecting you."

I nodded. We both stood up.

"I thought I could help," said Leo, his voice cracking. He cleared his throat.

"Well you're here now," he said evenly, and waved his hands for us to sit back down.

He took a seat in a leather chair opposite us, we sat down on the patterned sofa. I glanced around at the room. It was a funny place- had most of the things making a house a home- but was missing others things like family pictures and ornaments. This was somewhere for work only, not for family.

"A bad bit of business gents," he said.

"Can I just say first, I didn't know they were your men…" I started.

I stopped when he raised his hand and made a shushing noise. It took every inch of me to control my temper.

"No you can't," said Nine-mill belligerently, "I wanna know first why you were poking your nose into my fucking affairs."

"I don't understand Mr. Best," I said.

"I wanna know why you were round at Davy's place before that, sticking your neb in. I hear then you gave him a second visit and trashed the fucking place."

He spoke slowly, but assured, and as he did so, he leaned down and pulled out a case from underneath the sofa. He lifted up a cloth and began to polish the black leather exterior.

"I didn't do any warning off. I simply asked Davie if he would go easy on Big Stevie, who owed him some money. He said that was fine."

I took a breath and stopped and gestured with my hands. Nine-mill kept his eyes on his cleaning. I continued on, "Next thing I know and my shop's been broken into and there's two guys waiting inside for me. Bloody front door is wrecked."

He chewed the inside of his cheek and carried on polishing. He looked up and towards the back of the room,

"Perhaps breaking into your shop was a little heavy handed," he said, flashing a look towards Thin. He then returned his focus to the case, opening it up. I glanced back and winked at Thin.

"Davy tells me that the first time, you threatened him, then you came back and half wrecked his place. I can't allow that type of thing to go on."

"That's not true- we had an agreement the first time, I was only speaking up for a mate, he was actually good about it. Obviously I see now, he must have been lying." I shrugged, "Yeah, the second time, I lost my rag and made my point that I was pissed off. But only 'cause of what happened at my gaf."

"When you also beat up my men?" he said, lifting a nine millimetre rifle out of the case. He closed the case, set it on the ground and began to clean the rifle. It was 'the' 'nine-mill'. He was infamous for it- a garden gun some people call it; meant for killing vermin in the garden really. It wasn't what Bestie was infamous for using it for. Leo had been sitting patiently, playing the statesman of the family, he cut in then,

"I don't think Davie has been altogether honest with you Mr. Best. It seems that things just got out of hand and Davy's the one who pushed it that way. But yeah, I know Jim is sorry and like I said, things got out of hand."

"Yes they did," said Nine-mill, his voice raised and his eyes beginning to kindle beneath the emerald. They were the last thing that many dead men had seen. In an instant he calmed again and went back to his cleaning,

"It so happens that I have a financial issue with Davy also, and he is reliant apparently on a large figure coming from Stevie. You have caused problems with this, and disrespected my men at the same bloody time. I've also turned a blind eye to some of your other business dealings up until now," he said, raising an eyebrow.

"I'm sorry about your fellas," I said, trying to sound earnest, "hopefully you can understand my side. I was surprised by two guys breaking into my shop, what was I to do? But the thing with Davie- I don't understand what happened there. I'm sorry- it's not my place maybe- but I don't think Davy's being straight with you. And Stevie only owed him a few hundred quid."

He looked up sharply, when I said that. He returned once again to his cleaning,

"I've always liked Stevie," he said softly, "he's a good lad."

Suddenly his manner changed again,

"So you two think I'm a fucking idiot who's getting taken for a ride- is that it?" he said enraged.

"No, of course not," said Leo swiftly.

"No," I agreed.

He continued to clean the rifle, with harder movements now. I'm sure it was a tactic to intimidate and I've gotta admit it was working.

"Could we maybe have a private chat outside," said Leo, chipping in again, "I'd like to run something past you," he said, holding up two cigarettes.

There seemed like an endless pause, and then Nine-mill stood up abruptly and snatched a cig from his hand, and glared at me. They walked out together, silently. I sat there fidgeting; I never fucking fidget. I was like a coiled snake, but I couldn't afford to bite anybody else. I watched them through the glass; heavy in conversation, with plenty of hand gesturing on both sides. After five minutes or so, they came back inside.

"Okay Jim, fuck off then, "said Nine-mill as he walked back towards me. I stood up and noticed Thin looking confused at the back of the room. Leo shot me a discreet wink.

"Leo'll explain it to you. If you do a wee job for me, then we're all square- alright?"

"Fair enough, cheers Mr. Best," I said, relieved, but still feeling like I was kissing the headmaster's arse.

…

"What the fuck did you say to him?" I asked, back in the car and driving us out of the estate.

"You fucking owe me," said Leo, with a nervous laugh.

"Come on- what's the craic?"

"Well, basically, I already knew that things weren't all that rosy between Davy and him. I had heard that Davy owed him for something near ten grand. It turns out that Davy had spun some tall tale involving Stevie- all lies. Nine-mill pretty much knew already that it was all shite- you got lucky with that bit."

"So what've we gotta do?"

"Well- this could be the not so fun bit. Nine-mill's quite fond of Stevie anyway and he's heard that Davy has got him locked up- trying to rough him up…"

"What the fuck?" I spat, interrupting.

"I know. If he has him- it's against Nine-mill's orders. Seems to me that Davy has taken him more to shut him up."

"Fucksake! I'll fuckin' murder him!" I said, punching the dashboard.

"Hold on Michael Stone, Nine-mill wants us to find out if he's there and we can rough up Davy a bit if we like. Says he doesn't mind if we wreck the place too. Seems like it was all gonna kick off between them anyhow- just you and Stevie got tangled up in it. Could be that Davy's been thinking about even toppling Nine-mill. Personally I don't think he has the balls."

We turned out on to the carriageway and towards Ards. The daylight was beginning to fade.

"So, he wants to use us against Davy Dick and then if it all goes tits up- it's nothing to do with him?"

"Yeah exactly. You gotta remember there are still bigger men than Nine-mill and he can't be seen as overstepping the mark- even with wankers like Davy."

"Jeez- I owe you Leo, seriously mate. Stevie better be alright."

"You're family," he said and lit up another smoke.

"Fuck, I'll be having a proper smoke tonight," I said with a guffaw.

"Well you can't be getting too stoned- we're gonna have a job to do first."

Chapter 11

Leo dropped me back home and I had my dinner. I was in another daze. I couldn't even tell you what I ate. I tried to act normal, but I'm sure Pavla knew something was wrong, maybe Skye too. I had a beer with my tea and had a quick smoke after, then made my excuses and drove off to meet Leo, half a mile from Davy Dick's club. Pavla was pretty pissed at me, but I'd have to deal with that later on. I nearly tripped over her face on the way out the door.

"You're late," said Leo gruffly, standing by his car, down at the old bridge, smoking.

"Fucksake," I said, checking my watch, "It's not even ten after nine."

"Need I remind you that I'm doing you the favour?"

"Okay, okay, I'm sorry, I know."

We padded along the river bank, both dressed in black, each with a holdall on our backs. It was like old times. Well, I had been out of things a long time, I didn't know how often Leo got his hands dirty anymore. I didn't want to know either. Once we got to the car park, there weren't many cars left. We sat by the forest's edge, just beyond the crumbling outside wall. We waited. After an hour or so there were only two cars left in the car park.

"You ready?" asked Leo.

"Yep, let's fuckin' do it."

We each took out a balaclava and pulled them on.

...

Blood spurted out from his forehead after the first blow. The second one put him out. We had gone in the front door and found it unlocked. We had inched along the corridor and found one of Davy's Dick's dickheads. It was the back of my Glock that gave him the two blows (I wouldn't wanna mispronounce that out loud). Leo stepped back to the front door and snibbed it shut. We shoved tissue paper in the guy's mouth and tied him up with some fishing wire, leaving him in the corridor. We skulked on, guns raised, our breathing hot and laboured under the balaclavas. We searched the whole floor before silently heading towards Davy's office. There was no sign of anyone else for sure. We waited behind the heavy wooden door quietly and then Leo waved his thirty three, saying it was time to go in. I burst through and Davy looked like he near shit his pants. He was sitting alone at his desk. No new computer as yet.

"Christ," he shouted, flinching, "What the fuck is this?"

"You're gettin' robbed," Leo shouted back, stepping in behind me.

Davy's surprised face turned to fury, and more than that- cocky too.

"D'ya know who I am son?" he asked incredulously.

"Yeah, you're a dick," I said.

He looked fucking raging. Suddenly he lunged to open his desk drawer. I was only a few feet away and I didn't really want to shoot the bastard. I threw my gun with great force at his head. It made a thud and it struck and much more blood came out of him than from the first guy. He fell backwards off his chair and landed heavily on the deck. The sight of it made me laugh out loud. I controlled myself. Leo walked around the desk decisively and laid a kick into his ribs,

"Any more fucking about and you're gettin'shot! Right?" he said firmly.

Davy didn't answer and just looked indignant. I picked up my gun off the floor, flicked the safety off and held it to Davy's head.

"Where's Stevie?" I whispered into his ear hole.

Davy squirmed and then looked up questioningly- either at the question or the voice. Maybe they just fitted together.

"What?" he said simply.

"Where the fuck is Stevie?" I repeated.

"I know who you two are," he spat, looking at the ground.

"Maybe we better kill you now then," cut in Leo.

Davy blew out air and flicked his head, "He's downstairs".

"Show us," I said urgently, moving the gun away from his head.

"Right, 'mon then," he said, deflated; picking himself off the ground, "You'll be dead for this," he added, almost matter of fact.

"I don't think so," replied Leo.

"Other people won't be happy about this," tried Davy, walking round the table.

"I'm not sure about that either," said Leo.

We let Davy lead us down the stairs and into the basement. The hall light cast some light on the room and I could make out an old broken pool table, some chairs and empty kegs. He pulled another light switch, and then there was Stevie, illuminated in all his glory. He was tied to a chair in the middle of the room, his face bruised and smeared with old blood. He was only wearing a vest and a pair of boxers. He looked frigged. The boxers had a Union Jack on them. If they'd had a tricolour, Leo might have left him there.

When he set eyes on our masked faces, he first looked panicked.

"It's alright Stevie, we're here to help ya," I said.

"Jimmy, is that you?" he said excitedly, "thank fuck, get me out of this shit hole."

"No, that's not, I don't know who you're talking about," I said, sounding like a pillock, "But we're here to help ya." Davy let out a sarcastic snort. Leo gave him an abrupt shove; knocking him unceremoniously onto the dusty floor. I let another laugh slip out.

...

About half an hour later, Leo, me and Stevie were all standing at the edge of the car park- watching the club go up in flames. Davy and the other guy were next to us, tied up on the floor, with tissue in their mouths. They didn't look too pleased all in all. After we had dragged them outside, me and Leo had each thrown a petrol bomb into the club. I felt like a child again. All I was missing was a bottle of Bucky.

...

"You been smoking?" asked Pavla irately when I eventually got back home.

"Something like that," I said.

Things had kind of turned out okay. How was I to know what was coming? I didn't know I was gonna end up here. I still don't know how I got here. Anyway, I was on edge for a few weeks after, worrying about any retaliation from Davy. About a month later, I stopped worrying- when his body turned up in the river beside his club. One less dick in the world, I suppose.

...

Bongo Fury 2:
Holiday For Skins

Chapter 1

"The unidentified man was found by a member of the public, who had been out walking his dog along by the duck pond in Newtownards…"

I paused and looked up from the newspaper,

"Fuckin' hell love, they've found another one," I shouted across the kitchen to Pavla.

"Shhhhhh," she scolded, plucking Skye up from her high chair and covering her ears,

"She will repeat it Jim."

"Jeez", I said, rolling my eyes, "here, listen to this," I added, searching for the spot,

"The unnamed man's head was almost severed from his body and a large portion of skin had been removed from one of his fingers."

I looked up, shaking my head,

"Bloody hell, that's the third one."

"Ah-ah!" Pavla rasped sharply, then breezed out with Skye on her shoulder.

"I didn't say fuck," I called after her.

Chapter 2

I was gulping down my second coffee of the day when my first customer rolled in. It was near eleven. My mind had been drifting back to the morning paper, and I was thinking how there were some sick puppies about in this old world. Pav had put Skye down for a nap and we had breakfast together; she hadn't been really that pissed off with me. I made us my speciality scrambled eggs, with extra buttery toast, so she had to at least be civil. Anyways, I suppose I should introduce myself a little. No actually I won't; if you don't know who I am, you should have bought my first fucking book.

"Brian, how are you mate?"

"Not bad Jim, Baltic out there today buddy."

He wasn't actually a customer, so much as a salesperson, or even a stakeholder if you will. Brian helped me out with shifting some of my gear. Gear of the green variety. He pulled his tattered old 'Norn Iron' cap off and revealed his graying and slightly receding locks.

"Cuppa mate?" I asked.

"Always," he said, rubbing his hands.

After I had a brew with Brian, he took a few baggies to sell and headed on. I did a wee tidy up round the store, had a wipe round and that, which resulted in me mostly just strumming a couple of my best guitars. I tuned the sunburst Les Paul to DADGAD and tried a bit of 'Stairway to Heaven.' I fiddled about for a few minutes. It's a fucking embarrassment that I still can't nail the intro. Maybe it'd be easier in Open G. Fuck it. I set it down and decided to try and find the vacuum. The summer holidays were coming and I thought there'd hopefully be an increase in school kids coming in for strings and even a few records. Well, I was an optimist at least. It was also about a year after the whole thing with Davy Dick. God rest him- I suppose. A few more customers trickled in and out again. Most of them didn't buy anything- it fucking cracks me up. I thought about getting some tablature books in- just so I could say, 'This is not a library.' Anyway, all in all things were pretty sweet with my little life. The shop was surviving, people still needed me to sell them some grass, Skye had started playgroup, and Pav was nearly done with her NVQ or QCF thing. I still got to keep 'Bongo Fury'; my sanctum, my piece of- and peace from the world.

After dinner that night, I left my girls watching *In the Night Garden* and scooted out to see my brother Leo. Me and him had been meeting up more regularly again, having a few drinks like brothers are meant to.

"Pint?" I asked unnecessarily.

"Cheers Jim, I'll get us a wee short to go with it."

"Okay, I better leave my fucking car then," I said and turned to the waitress, "Two Harps please love."

We decided to hook up in Wolseys- neither of us had gone there in years, taking our drinks to a corner snug. We had found ourselves in the habit of going to places where Leo shouldn't be too likely to bump into 'work colleagues.' He had risen up the ranks a brave bit recently and from what I gathered, he had quite a bit of responsibility. I tried not to ask too many questions- I didn't much want to know. We got comfy and I threw my coat over the back of the booth. My ears pricked up to the sounds of some early Prince coming over the bar speakers. Involuntarily, my head started to bob.

"Bloody new suit again brother," I said, taking my first cool and satisfyingly bubbly sip.

"Surprised you'd notice, you scruffy bastard," he responded, smirking.

I looked down at my Led Zep T-shirt and 'go-to' blue jeans. I shrugged. He was in a full blue suit, striped, with a tie and everything. Until recently I had only caught him in a full tie and suit at funerals- or in court. On reflection, both had been reasonably regular occurrences.

"How's your clan?" I asked.

"Jesus," he said with a shake, "bloody kids, if I have to go to one more teacher meeting about Blake's behaviour."

He pulled at his tie and took a long slug.

We talked for a bit about the kids, Bongo Fury; the usual shit. He seemed in good form, calm, not too sarky. The moody bastard was in good form. That restless spirit of his seemed to be finally settling down a bit too. Fair play to him I reckoned.

"We'll have to get a wee night out with the wives- get babysitters- no kids," he added, starting on his short. He had bought us both a Black Bush.

"Absolutely- just say when, things are pretty quiet our end."

"Yeah actually," he said, pulling at his tie again, with his forehead creasing, "Things are a wee touch mad at the minute- I've some business shit to get sorted out- it'll be better in a wee bit. Might need to leave it a week or two."

"Dead on- just when suits," I said.

"Fuck, this place sure has changed, hasn't it?" said Leo, looking round, "They've done it up- must have cost some."

"Yeah," I said, following where his gaze had rested, "It used to be dark and a bit friggen dingy," I added, then emptying my glass, "It was better like that."

He tutted

"Well- 'nother round?" I enquired.

"Go on- a short for me. Just going for a smoke," he said rising, slipping out of the booth and then checking his phone. He made a face, then shuffled on outside.

Chapter 3

I was greeted by newly hung bunting on my way into work the next day. Union flags and UVF banners had sprung up- engulfing the estates and everywhere in between. It was if I was Union Jack himself and they had been put out for my birthday. Maybe it was a present from my brother. The thought made me smile. We were approaching July and the period where hard core Prods felt the need to piss all over their territory. I'm a Unionist, many in my family have fucking died for being Unionists; I'm more connected that a fucking Connect-4. But, to me, I think 'fucking easy on boyos.' I like The Union, but I like The Beatles too. I just don't feel the need to drape Beatles flags outside my house, and my neighbours' house, and to set fire to flags of The Rolling Stones.

It was already nine when I got to my shop, take-out coffee in hand. Two men in grey suits were standing outside my shutter. I had been late before, but had never found customers waiting on me. I slowed my steps and eyed them as I rustled in my pockets for my keys. The first man was stocky, chewing hard on some gum, making a face like the gum tasted of aniseed. I bloody hate aniseed. The second was a touch older, taller and leaner. He nodded and gave me a sideways smile.

"Ahh," I said dramatically, "You two must be queuing for the 'One Direction' tickets, isn't it great that the lads are back together?"

I started to pull up the shutter, almost shoving 'Sour Face' out the way. The second man kept smiling,

"Hello Jimmy, very droll, we'd like a word in your ear."

"Certainly," I said, opening the inside door, "Come through, I am here for all your vinyl and musical instrument queries."

I switched on the lights and walked through, then positioned myself behind the counter. It felt better there, I was in charge whatever this was, it was my shop after all. The last time two fellas came in like this, I smashed a pink ukulele over one of their thick heads. I let these two amble in behind me.

"We're police, this…"

"No shit," I interrupted, offering up my finest unimpressed face.

"I am D.I Merritt, this is D.S Timmons," he continued passively.

I shrugged and let out a yawn.

"Look, is there somewhere quiet we can go?" broke in Timmons.

"Is it not quiet enough here? It's not my busy time," I added and shot him a sarcastic smile.

"Fine," said Merritt, his patience dwindling a touch, "It's up to you. It's also up to you if we arrest you for possession and sale of a Class B drug.

"I don't know what you're talking about," I answered, far too quickly.

"C'man Jimmy, don't fuck around," began Timmons aggressively, "We haven't the time for it."

Timmons' face had started to purple. Merritt creased his forehead at his colleague, then returned his gaze to me,

"We know all about your plants. What have you got- three, four of them? We don't care much, but we will, if you don't do a little something for us."

"I don't now what you're talking about, "I said again, controlled this time, "And you," I added louder, waggling my big finger at Timmons, "Calm the fuck down."

"Fuck up Black," Timmons shot back sulkily, kicking the floor with his toe cap.

"Get out of my fuckin' face!" I said, losing it slightly, and stepping towards the side of the counter.

"Alright, enough!" said Merritt firmly; I think as much to Timmons, as to me.

"Okay, I don't know what yous are fucking talkin' about, but say what yous came to say," I offered, placing my hands flat on the counter. I could see drops of perspiration forming and I hoped they didn't notice.

"We just want some information Jimmy, that's all," said Merritt smoothly, starting his pitch.

"You're in a pretty unique position," chimed in Timmons, trying a less hostile tone and tac, "We know you're not paramilitary, and the most you do is sell a little grass, knock out a few dickheads once in a while. But your family."

He left that there.

"What about my fucking family?" I asked, my patience starting to fail again.

I was a bit rattled too. They were still cops after all- and they had some dirt on me, so I'd have to try and keep my cool.

Merritt took over again,

"Look, we're not going to ask you to betray anyone or anything like that," he said, gesturing heavily, "we're not interested in you family as such. We know who they are, but that's not what this is about."

I admit I was baffled about what they did want. It could have been the adrenaline shooting through me, disabling my thought processing, but I was bloody confused. And worried. What kind of a shake down was this?

"What do you fucking want then?" I asked quietly.

"Jimmy," started Merritt, leaning against the counter, talking as if we were two old acquaintances; shooting the shit in the bar, "Do you read the papers?"

Chapter 4

I shut the shop up when it got to lunch time. I took a half an hour over at The Pitstop Café, up off the Rathgael Road roundabout. I mechanically wolfed down my seven piece fry, thinking about the two peelers from earlier on. They had gone on to say how they were investigating some recent murders, all taking place around Belfast and North Down. I had read about two lads in recent weeks getting killed and I knew that both had been connected. I thought that had been a coincidence or just some infighting with the boyos. Details about the third body hadn't been released yet. What connected all three was the fact that each man had had a large part of skin peeled off from one of their fingers. It could have been down to torture, but the funny thing was that the fucker had removed it post mortem.

"You're not to go telling anyone this," Merritt had said, lowering his voice, "The most recent murder is of Bestie Nine-mill."

I had been genuinely shocked and it takes a lot to fucking shock me.

My instinct was to smile for some reason,

"No fucking way. I hear Bestie is over in England anyway. He's been doing some business deal or something," I shrugged then, "You know, ya hear things. Nobody's gonna take out Bestie "

Merritt regarded me coldly and shook his head, "It's definitely him, it all checks out. DNA, you name it. It took a while to be sure- his head was near ripped off and the rest of him wasn't great looking either."

"Fucking hell," I had said, leaning back from the counter, "It can't be him," I looked at the floor, "He's meant to be over on business surely? Who'd be stupid enough? He could be negotiating for the DUP with the Tories for all I know- but no one would be stupid enough to off him. They'd have all the boys out after them."

"Well someone fucking did," broke in Timmons, looking all pleased with himself.

I regarded him coolly, like a toddler who's just thrown his food at you.

"Fuck off Tiny Tim," I said.

...

I played around with the last of my fried egg, prodding it with my fork, and reflected on how there was almost a scuffle between me and Timmons. Merritt had kept things calm. It wouldn't have done well to assault an officer of the law, on top of whatever else they knew about. I don't know why I got angry, I didn't particularly care for Nine-mill. I suppose I respected him in a way. He was part of the old school institution; he commanded your respect or he'd commandeer your knees. I thought back to the day me and my brother had sat next to him, as he threateningly polished that gun of his. I was just surprised that someone had the nerve to hit him. I set my fork down and thought back to watching them leave my shop, relief having brushed over me. A lonesome customer had sauntered in, then they quietly told me they'd be in touch and that all I had to do was keep my ears open, and gently push a few questions around here and there. I told them I could do that. What else could I do, except go to jail?

I sat back in the hard wooden chair and readied myself to go back to work. I became aware of two young girls, chatting at a table near by. To be fair, I could best describe them as a couple of wee millies.

"You going out the night Carly?" asked the first one, broad as you like.

"No money. Spent all my spares on this here," said the other, grabbing her own peroxide curls with a scowl,

"Fuckin' disgrace, themins are usually good. My heart's broke"

"Who done it for ya love- Stevie Wonder?"

I let out a smile, the old ones are the best.

Anyway, I wanted to know what these murders were all about and I was happy to do a bit of digging for them. I just wouldn't necessarily tell them whatever I found out.

Chapter 5

"Rub my feet," said Pavla.

"No, you've got hairy toes," I replied.

She bounced up from our huddle on the sofa.

"I fucking do not!" she protested, slapping my arm.

"I'm only gegging love," I said, "Make me a cuppa?"

"You can get me a bloody tea," she said, pouting. When she said 'bloody', it sounded somewhere in between Yorkshire and South Africa. I found it endearing. I'm a big softie.

"If you switch off this fucking Love Island bullshit I will."

She considered this.

"We could watch a movie?"

"Deal," I said.

While the kettle was boiling, I made a phone call.

"How you doing Jimmy?" Leo said, answering after a few rings.

"Not bad buddy, look, are we okay talking on this line?"

"Yeah, should be fine," he said sounding hesitant, "Just don't go confessing to anything much; like killing J.F.K... or J.R."

"Yeah, okay, look," I said, pacing out of the kitchen and into the hall as the kettle began to hiss too noisily, "I've got some info for ya. You know that body that turned up a couple of days ago- had the fucked up finger?"

"Yeah, uhuh" he said gruffly.

"I've been told that it's Bestie Nine-mill."

He went silent for a moment and I paused, licking my lips.

"Bestie's meant to be in England. You sure?" he asked quietly.

"Yeah, my guy is reliable."

Me and Leo weren't really all that close and I wasn't about to tell him that I was talking to the cops.

"Fuck," he said simply.

"I know. I thought you'd want to know."

"Yeah, yeah, thanks Jim," he said absently, "Who told you?"

"I'm sorry, I can't tell ya Leo."

"Aww c'mon, for fucksake," he said, more pleading than angry.

"I can't, I'm sorry. Will this mean much hassle for you?"

"I suppose. Yeah, if it's definitely right. Shit."

There was an awkward pause.

"Well thanks Jim, here I'd better go make a few calls."

"Okay, no probs. You didn't hear it from me- okay?"

"Okay Jim, I'll ring you again, cheers."

"Alright Leo, see you later."

That was done, I'd keep the fuzz sweet, might as well try and forget about it. Things would be alright. I brought in a bottle of wine with the teas and a couple of DVD's. Pavla looked up at me, looking pleased, then suspicious.

"We're not having sex tonight," she said.

Chapter 6

I put an inaccurate 'Back in 5 minutes' sign on the shop door and drove up to Shorter's Garage in Ards, about eleven the next morning. My buddy Benny was a mechanic there.

"Bout ya Jim," he said, his gnarly, oil stained paw grabbing my hand.

"How you doing Benny, mate?" I replied.

The hairy man mountain made even me look undersized.

"You time for a chat?" I asked.

"Yeah, he said," scratching at his unkempt beard, leaving an oily residue behind, "I'm on my own today, Big Wayno's off on his holidays. He's gettin' an early bit of wreckin' in before the twelfth," Benny added, with a throaty chuckle.

...

He made us a cup of char and we sat on two old wooden sun chairs out on the front gravel. It was a dundering in old garage, up a steep path by the new industrial estate. The 'Shorter's Garage' sign had long lost a G and an A, but Benny assured me they both like it better that way. The sun was out and I squinted as I flicked ash from my cigarette into his big plastic ash tray. It said 'Smithwicks' on it, which was only just legible, beneath the oily grime. I wondered how many years had gone by since one of them had swiped it from some rathole or another. We chatted for a bit and then I got down to business. Benny and his boss had fixed up cars nice and quiet for the boys for years- whatever needed doing before or after some dodgyness. Benny had gotten friendly with a lot of them too and I know he met up socially now and again. He just wasn't a paramilitary as such- I suppose a wee bit like myself.

"So here, I'm looking into something for a mate," I began, "It's to do with these murders, 'yon ones with the fucked up fingers."

Benny's big brown eyes seemed to glaze over for a moment and look past me.

"Yeah it's pretty mad that whole thing," he agreed and blew out his cheeks.

He didn't take the cue.

"I wanted to see if you knew anything?" I pushed, giving a shrug.

He lifted his tea and swigged it back and ran his hand through his thick hair, revealing a few greys.

"Sorry Jim- haven't heard nothin'. It sure is a weird one."

I looked at him squarely,

"Ya know they found another one a few days back? Haven't said who it is yet though."

"Have they? I hadn't heard."

I looked at him, hadn't heard? It was the fucking talk of the town.

"Yeah, it's all a wee bit feckin' grim," I said, "But if you hear anything?"

"Sure Jim, course," he replied, trying to sound enthusiastic, "no bother bud."

Maybe he just didn't like getting involved in that kind of shit or he didn't want me carrying anything back to me bro. It was just a bit weird.

"Cheers Benny, that'd be sweet."

"Better be getting back Jim," he said, getting heavily to his feet.

"Okay."

Chapter 7

That night was uneventful- for me anyway. I slept contentedly enough, but during my sleep, unbeknownst to me, a voicemail was left on my phone. I didn't get it till the next morning. It was from my old mate Stevie. He didn't sound himself;

"Jim, it's me mate. I gotta speak to you about something...look, it's not good. I can't talk on this thing- look ring me- tonight if you can. See ya."

Later that day I found out that he was dead.

Chapter 8

"What'dya mean he's dead? Are you fuckin' messing with me?"

Timmons didn't react as I got up in his face, he actually looked a little sorry for me this time.

Merrit cut in between us again and said,

"I know yous two were mates. I'm sorry. We need to get the bastard who's doing this."

My breathing felt heavy and I had to force myself to calm the fuck down. That's how I found out; from those two. They soon drifted out again, then there was a haze, and the rest of the morning was a blur. I locked the shop door and sat inside and cried.

"I'm sorry love, I'm sorry," is what I can remember Pav saying to me later that day, stroking my arm.

We just sat that afternoon in our front room, huddled up on the sofa. He was one of my best mates and he was dead. Not just dead, and not even just murdered. He was fucking beaten, his throat cut and the skin from one of his fingers removed. I just sat there and let her stroke me and I let the pain lap up from inside me and spill out, just a little. But what I promised myself right there, was that I would find the bastard responsible and I would make him sorry. I'd also make him say he was sorry, and then I'd kill him.

Chapter 9

Three weeks passed and 'The Twelfth' passed too. It went off peacefully enough- well, as peacefully as you can ever expect it to. I had spent much of my spare time taking to old friends and acquaintances, trying to find some link between the murders. Most seemed to have no idea or pretended not to. All the talk was about who had killed Bestie Nine-mill. Every day, the T.V news and local papers had something about his death. The rest of the dead were overshadowed; including my best mate.

"What's with the tabloids sayin' that the murders aren't really linked, and that the finger cutting could just be a new paramilitary trend- like sending a message or something?" I asked.

"I don't know Jim, I can't tell them what to write or broadcast. But, I'd prefer they didn't think they were linked anyhow," said Merritt soberly.

They had let me alone for a week or two, but had called in early again one morning. I guess they'd figured I'd had long enough to grieve. Or perhaps just the right amount.

"You're not startin' to think they're not?" I continued.

"No, of course they're linked," said Timmons, shaking his head dismissively.

I glared at him, "So why do yous care about the press?"

"I don't want the public to panic," Merritt said plainly, holding his hands up. He began to pace and then lifted up a few records from the shelf and started to shuffle them into a neater position, "They most definitely are linked and not just that- they're all done by the same person."

He looked at me absently, then his brow creased.

"How can you be sure? Like DNA?" I asked.

"No, not that. They haven't left any trace of anything. He's thorough."

"Just take our word for it, for fucksake," barged in Timmons irately."

"Fuckin' bell end," I muttered under my breath, not rising to it this time.

"There's no doubt it's one killer Jimmy," continued Merritt, "All of our experts are certain. But beyond that- we just have no idea who he is."

Merritt caught his subordinate's eye and then looked away again. His voice was quieter;

"Jim, I shouldn't be tellin' you this much, but we need all the help we can get. We're gonna need more from you."

"I've been tryin'. I've been tryin' everywhere. I wanna get the fucking fella," I shouted, emotions rising up again. I forced them down.

He stopped and examined my face.

"Alright, I hear you. I just think that this guy will go on and on. Listen Jim," he paused, "We have a lot of experts working on this. All sorts of guys. They tell me he's a serial killer."

He let it sit a moment. He paused and glanced at Timmons again, Timmons's own face offered nothing.

"They tell me that this guy is most definitely a serial killer. That's dangerous. They tell me he's clever- that's very dangerous. But I know he can be caught- just like anyone else. But, they tell me he doesn't leave any clues. We've got basically nothin'. All we have is that all of the deaths involve guys involved with paramilitaries. What I don't know is why."

Chapter 10

"It's been too long again Jim," my brother said, shifting himself into the booth.

This time we had chosen The Goat's Toe in Bangor. It was the first I'd seen him since Stevie's funeral.

"It has," I agreed, and sipped my Harp, while scrutinising his face. I was pretty pissed off that he hadn't made much of an effort.

We were up on the roof garden and it was just starting to get busy. We sat at the long drinks table, up from the converted caravan-come smoking shelter. It was pretty cool. I kept looking at him, I didn't have anything to say.

"What?" he said, gesturing defensively, but letting out a laugh.

"It's nathin' much," I said.

Truth be told, I didn't quite know what exactly was bothering me, or what I was really thinking about.

"Look, I know I should have made more time for ya," he said, squirming on the hard wood, "but since the whole Nine-mill thing came out- things have been hectic."

"I'm sure," I said, "I understand Lee," my voice softening, "would just like to see you more now and again."

"I know, and you will. I think things'll settle down soon," he said, and undid the buttons on his jacket. His beer paunch became more visible beneath his wrinkled shirt.

"Another new jacket?" I asked, raising an obvious eyebrow.

"It is- so what- 'bout time you smartened up- like I said the last time."

"Feck aff," I said and lit up a smoke.

Leo followed suit.

"But yeah, I have bought some new threads. Truth is that Nine-mill's death," he paused and lowered his voice, "his death had got me what you'd say are a few 'promotions.' I wasn't lookin' for them though, just how it goes. Means I'm busier."

"How you findin' it?"

"Alright. It's going okay- just a lot to sort out at the moment. The guys a few rungs up are clambering over each other- if ya know what I mean?"

"Yeah."

"I'm happy just to sit tight and keep my head down."

89

He sucked hard on his cigarette, and gazed beyond the beer garden and out towards the two sets of church spires. The quiet moment was interrupted when a drunk, two tables up; fell of his stool and crashed down onto the floor. There was a hush as he clambered to stand up and then as an afterthought; he gave a little bow.

"Yeoooo," followed a loud a roar from the surrounding rabble.

"Twat," I whispered to Leo.

The next hour or two passed quietly enough. The only further excitement was when some huffy bit threw her engagement ring at her boyfriend. It dropped down beneath the decking and all drama broke loose. A manager with a hammer and a screwdriver didn't manage to rectify it, and the unhappy couple were told they'd have to wait until Monday to try and get it back. Leo winked at me as they ambled down the aisle past us and left. We both were half liquored up by then and I spun the conversation round more directly to the murders. I suppose I wanted to pump him a bit for any info.

"So what's your take on it? Who the fuck do you think did it?" I asked, leaning in.

"Shit, I really dunno," he said, having difficulty getting his lighter to spark up another smoke, "It's really weird. All I can think of dat some dickheads from the other group are trying to push us. Take down the big dog ya'know? I just don't know why they haven't owned up yet. Could be they're planning another big move. Fuck 'em. Fuck da lot of 'em! We've got our own plans though Jim," he said, and looked hazily satisfied.

I don't know if it was his cig finally catching or something else.

We shared a taxi home around midnight and it dropped him off first.

"Out towards Scrabo," I said to the driver as he pulled away from Leo's house, after our drunken farewells.

I watched Leo as he struggled down the path to his house. He took out his mobile to make a phone call as he approached his front step. I shook my head and watched the trees and gates pass quickly, as the driver nipped up to a full thirty, back up the cul-de-sac. It always feels faster in the dark and the quiet of night. There's something about being all lit up within the dark too; more exposed.

"Stop here please mate," I blurted out abruptly, just before the turn at the end.

"You alright mate?" asked the driver.

"Yeah, just a bit sick, I uh, can take it from here- keep the change."

I bundled him a fiver and got out. As he sped off I started to amble slowly, but determinedly, back towards Leo's.

What was I doing? What did I want to ask him? Did I think Leo had something to do with things?

Did I think my brother was a serial killer?

No- he was many things, but not that. Yeah- he had actually probably killed people- but not like that. But something wasn't right. I knew that. I knew him- I'd known his lies and his tells since we were boys, running around the estate. He was hiding something. As I closed the gap, I felt my sweat becoming sticky in the pits of my T-shirt. I stopped by a tree, two doors before his house, in the most discreet position I could think of. I didn't exactly have all my wits about me. I lit up a cigarette and waited. What was I waiting for? I soon felt too cold, tired and stupid. I realised the drink had gotten the better of me and that I getting on like I was a bargain basement Humphrey Bogart chasing a Malteser Falcon. I turned to go and almost hit straight into the body stepping quickly towards me.

"What are ya hanging around out here for?" demanded a gravely, Antrim gulder.

"What the fuck is it to you?" I snarled back to the bulldog face that was barking at me.

He looked stocky and tight, but I was the size of an Irish Hound compared to him.

His eyes were flaring, but then suddenly uncertain.

"Fucksake Jimmy, it's you."

I squinted hard at the now smiling face.

"Jesus, Freddie Workman," I said realising who it was.

"Sorry Jim- just saw someone hanging about and had to check. How the hell are ya?"

"You're grand, good to see you- it must be, what?"

"… six years. Well that's how long I was inside any road."

"Shit- so you doing security for my big bro?"

"Aye, yeah, that's it. I've been out a few months now- meant to look you up."

"No bother- look I better get headin' on- fuckin' steaming."

"What you doing out here anyway Jim," he asked, as I went to go past him, his eyes questioning again.

"Aww, we had been out for drinks and the taxi was making me feel sick, so I hopped out. Just catching my breath. Didn't wanna puke on the guy's seat."

"Shit, well sure I'll just say to Leo and then I'll run you home."

"No, no, I'm alright" I said and patted him firmly on the arm.

I turned and started up the road,

"Good to see you Freddie. The walk'll do me good, see you about," I said, turning on my heel to look at him.

"Alright Jim, sure thing," he said.

Chapter 11

"Hello?" I said into my phone, not recognising the number.

"Hello Jim."

I was sitting in 'Subway' the next morning, treating myself to a sausage bap and flat white.

"Is that you Benny?"

"Yeah," he continued, flatter than my flat white, "Listen Jim, I was thinkin' 'bout Stevie and everything and I... shit," he said pausing, "Fuck Jim, I shouldn't be talkin' to you."

I sat up straight and pushed my sarnie to one side.

"Benny," I said calmly, "Anything you tell me- I appreciate it and here- I won't say fuck all to anyone." I waited as he breathed out a couple of times.

"Okay, right, I'm sayin' nuthin' more than this and I don't know nuthin' for definite. I've got no proof, just some things I've heard. I'm just giving you a name. After that, I'd best not talk to ya for a while okay?"

"Okay, thank you Benny, tell me," I said, trying to hold my nerve.

"Freddie Workman," he said and hung up.

I sat there looking at the stem rising off my coffee and a thin smile crept over my face. I don't know why.

The rest of the day flew in and for some reason I felt better than I had done in weeks. I shouldn't have really- if it was Freddie who was killing people- then my brother was probably involved too, or at least knew about it. Pavla made a stir fry for tea and I gobbled it up, along with a couple of tinnies. We got Skye bathed and down and the pair of us collapsed on the sofa, in front of an old repeat of 'Friends.' We half watched it, holding hands, Pav playing around on Facebook, as the cast played exaggerated versions of the characters they had played a few seasons before.

"I'm sorry if I'm been a moody bastard recently," I said. She considered me and her eyes softened, as she rubbed up my arm.

"No Jimmy, you lost your friend."

I nodded.

"I love you," I said into her ear.

"I love you," she echoed back.

"Want me to make you some tea?" I asked.

"No, I need to send a few messages, I'll have one in a while, thank you baby."

"Okay, I'm gonna pop up for a quick smoke, be down in half an hour."

"Okay," she said, returning my smile. I sat down with a piece of paper and a pen. I stuck a spliff in my mouth and fired on a side of Lee Morgan on the record player. I felt like fucking Carrie in Homeland. I scribbled some notes down as I tried to gather my thoughts. Could I be sure? What made most sense? I put those thoughts to the side for a moment and pictured my fists pummelling Workman's face into oblivion. I finished my smoke and then chewed on my pen. I had spent much of the afternoon in the shop, on the phone. I had rung a few particular mates, giving them various excuses and innocently dropped in a few questions about Workman. It seemed he had been out of prison for only a few months. That had correlated with the first murder. Seemingly he had been around about Belfast during all the murders, so he had been in the right place to have done it. There was also a lot of talk about his violence and sometimes taking things too far. He couldn't be relied on for punishment beatings anymore- got carried away and that sort of thing. Then there's Benny giving me his name too- I just didn't know any of the whys. Why the killings? Well, according to Merritt whoever the murderer was- he was probably a psychopath. Why did I suspect my brother too? And what of? Was he using a psycho for his own ends? I finished another smoke and lit up a third. I checked the clock- best get back to Pavla soon. So- what- my bro was up to his neck in this? Yeah- that's exactly what I was thinking. Why not? Something was different about Leo. His reactions weren't quite right on a number of things. But what did that we really tell me? Hardly enough to give to the cops.

'Search for a new land' came to an end and I lifted the vinyl and carefully put it back in its sleeve. He was the one who seemed to be benefiting from it all. But where did that leave me? What would I do anyway- give my brother to the police? A paramilitary big shot at that. Put my family at risk too? Fuck no.

After we watched a movie, Pav went off to bed and I said I'd stay up a while. My mind was still racing. It was only after eleven and I thought I'd sink a few pints at my local before bed. It took five minutes for me to be in Silver's, with a pint of Guinness settling nicely in front of me. It was a dank hole, but a homely one. I greeted a few regulars I knew and then got stuck into my stout. Me and the two either side didn't speak until Big Paul with the ruddy face beside me shouted loudly to the barman,

"Cheers Phil, see you tomorrow," and then ambled out.

He always did that. He never said fuck all to anyone-but always gave a loud goodbye like the life and soul. I sat on for another one and there were only a few of us left in the bar. I knew them all more or less. There was a young guy working the bar, hadn't been there long- think it was Andy you called him.

"Gimme a mix," demanded a voice behind me. It was Raymond. He's alright- but a bit of twat when he's had a skinful.

"Sorry what's that?" said the kid politely.

"Gimme a mix," said Raymond, nastier and more slurred than before. He was big brute in his forties like me, though even more out of shape.

"I'm sorry what's in it?" tried the awkward teen again.

"Fucksake, he doesn't know how to pour fucking drinks," went off Ray, trying to get a laugh from someone, but not succeeding, "Get me someone who can make me a fuckin'drink," he added, getting his real nasty face on.

I stood up sharply,

"Excuse me buddy," I said to the kid, making sure he knew I was being friendly, "This prick wants a stupid fucking ladies drink of Bacardi and Vat 19, no ice and with a diet coke."

I paused to look at Ray and he started to fume. I smiled at him, but shot him a look to let him know I would be ready to fucking rumble. I continued to move behind the bar and started to fix his drink, this got a smile from the kid and a couple of laughs from the drunks in the room.

"There we are," I said, slapping it down on the bar and setting a crisp fiver beside it, "On me."

I went to return to my seat and then waggled my forefinger dramatically,

"Oh yeah, needs stirred," I said and stuck my finger in and gave it a good stir. I licked it dry and then went back to my chair.

He looked raging, but just grabbed the drink and skulked off to a corner with it. Fuck 'em.

Chapter 12

It bucketed constantly the next day. Feckin' pissing it down. When I just nipped out from the shop for fags, I got a soaking. Most of the customers that day were in sheltering from the rain and pretending they weren't; examining guitars and feigning an interest in some record sleeves. I sent an occasional glare and they sauntered out again, hoods up. I struggled with what to do all day. I had said nothing to Pav. What could I say without scaring her? 'By the way- I might be getting busted for dealing drugs you don't know about?' 'My brother might be mixed up with some serial killings?' Frig that. I got to the point in my head where I knew I couldn't wade in with my brother or Workman, without it ending shitty. I couldn't dig around much more either, without drawing attention. I also wasn't gonna tout on my brother. But I did want to be in the clear and I wanted something done about Stevie's death. So, it wasn't much of a jump to figure I'd offer the police what I knew, try and keep Leo out of it and take it from there. It seemed the best thing I could do.

"Hello Jimmy, I hope you have something for me."
"Yeah I do, as it goes."

"Good, 'cause I'm sorry but this offer won't last forever."

I felt impatient. I was the one ringing him.

"I fucking know who it is," I said and left it hanging.

"We should meet then," Merritt replied evenly.

"You wanna come by my shop after closing?"

"Aye, that'd to alright," he said, I thought trying to hide the extent of his interest, "So, how sure are you?"

"Pretty sure. Listen, I've got a lot of info for ya. But I want guarantees in return. I want nothin' coming back on me or my family, goes for my brother too."

"Hold your horses son," Merritt said firmly, his voice growing louder and more assured, "Let's just see what you have and we'll take it from there. We'll be the ones offering the deals- not you."

I bit on my lip,

"Well, just come by yourself anyway, don't be bringing that prick Timmons."

"Anything else?" he replied sarcastically, "Jesus Jimmy, you should be glad if I don't turn up with three squad cars and haul you in for questioning. Anyway, Timmons is a good man- asked 'specially to work on this case in the first place."

I didn't respond one way or the other and just blew out some air. Eventually he seemed to figure that was all my response was going to be.

"I was gonna ring you later anyway," he continued, "thought you might be interested in something. Let's keep things friendly- okay?"

"Yeah- 'course."

"Your old mate Davy Dick. When our team checked back on other loyalist murders, turns out he had had the skin taken off a finger too."

"Oh right?"

"Yeah. Maybe this was our guy's first one. Anyway, there it is. Right, your shop it is. See ya later, don't let me down," he said and rung off.

I sat and drummed my fingers on the counter, watching big rain drops bounce off my front window. I tried to keep in time with the falling droplets. I was spacing out. I set down the phone and ran my hand over my head. Something didn't feel right. Something was coming. I went and made a coffee and wolfed down a Wispa. That helped a bit. I went back to watching the rain. After a while it started to ease, but the hazy grey outside began to cover everywhere instead.

'Fuck,' I said out loud to myself, jolting. I remembered; Workman would have still been in jail when Davy was murdered.

Chapter 13

It had turned into a cool and dark summer's night by the time I locked the door. The rain lessoned, but seemed still to be falling in huge, slow drops. I sat and waited. When the outline appeared against the shop door and the bang on the glass followed, something looked wrong about it. I pulled the door open and was greeted by Timmons's hardened grimace.

"I wasn't expecting you," I said.

"I bet you weren't," he replied and pushed past, both his hands pressed deep down inside his raincoat.

I closed the door behind us and left the gentle splashing of the overflowing guttering to continue alone outside. I turned to see Timmons beginning to drip dry. His eyes were dancing wildly in his head. Oh yeah, in his right hand was a '38.

Chapter 14

"No fucking need that for that," I said, with a harder voice than was good for me.

"Stand over there," he commanded, gesturing to the space on the wall between some guitars on stands and a stacked up new Gretsch kit.

"I was expecting your partner," I said, my mind whirring inside my head.

I walked over slowly and turned, then leaned my back against the wall.

"Yeah, he's not gonna make it," he said, his eyes now boring into me, bulbous in their sockets.

I could feel my mind slowing in its revolutions, trying to make sense of this, clicking through spaces, trying to find something that fitted, searching to understand.

"There's no need for the gun, put it away and we can talk," I offered lightly.

"I don't think so," he said and his eyes darted about him, sizing the place up, "So, you know who's been killing the paramilitary scum do you? Well, well. And you told Meritt that I shouldn't come along?"

"Well, not exactly…" I said, my eyes narrowing.

"Quiet," he instructed, and tightened his grip on the gun for a moment, he licked his lips, "Your fucking brother spilled to you then I suppose, did he? Not such a big man after all," he shouted, though his voice quivered.

I said nothing. But I felt what I admit was akin to horror. I had inadvertently pissed of a psychopath and made him come to my shop to silence me.

"Wanker," I said quietly.

"What you fuckin' say?" he snapped and stepped closer. I could smell something foul on his breath.

"I said wanker. Not you- me. I'm a fucking wanker."

"Fuck off."

I wasn't really certain what I was doing- I was probably a bit wired with the whole situation.

"I'm a wanker," I continued, "I seem to have made you think I knew it was you. Funny thing is; I didn't. I though it was someone else."

"Bullshit," he rasped.

"It's actually true," I went on. Looking back- I suppose I was trying to rile him up, or just buy some time to think,

"That's what I was gonna tell Merritt. Where is Merritt by the way?"

His eyes almost rolled in his head and he shook his hair from near his eyes in a twitch, "You won't be talking to Merritt again," he said softly.

My face must have dropped.

"Your fault though Black!" he screamed suddenly, "He was a decent man."

I just nodded, understanding what he meant.

"It was Leo told you," he said in a whisper, pointing at me with his other hand, his head nodding to himself. A big finger hung inches from my face, as accusatory as Banquo's himself, "Well he'll be coming here soon too, and we'll see what's what, get this all cleared up." He squinted up his eyes and rocked back on his heels. I chose my moment and suddenly scrambled down, grabbed the snare drum from the pile and heaved it into his face. It sent him flying back away from me. I would have preferred if it had been a bongo, but hey. It rattled and crashed as it rolled away, like a drunken drum roll. He regained his balance and the bugger managed to still keep the gun in his hand. I lunged at him, both my arms grabbing and batting down on his gun arm. I switched to punching his arm with my right fist and he let out a yelp, but came swinging back with his own right into my jaw. Fortunately he dropped the gun at the same time and I was able to take his punch easily enough. But then he rained down many more punches on me, like a Gorilla I had nicked a banana off of. I went down.

I'm sure I could feel his sweat and spittle too, as I put my arms up in defence to the ferocity, trying to regain my balance on the floor. It was hurting, but I knew this angry tirade would ease as he tired. It seemed like an eternity as I felt new gashes opening up across my head and shoulders. But then he tired. I dragged myself up and grappled with him, trying to off balance him and gain the upper hand again. He stumbled backwards and the rage in his eyes also flickered fear. He tripped again and then I went to work. Right, right, right, left, right, left. Each one hit home hard and Timmons began to sway. He backed away, towards the vinyl shelves and couldn't get a proper block up. His nose was pissing blood all over the place. I kept on, my pulse raging through my body, exhilarated; right, right, left, right. He finally staggered badly and fell back against a shelf of records. Luckily there wasn't much good stuff on it. If he had fallen on my new Blue Note reissues- I'd have finished him. He lay on the ground, breathing hard; bleeding, and barely conscious. I allowed myself a second to breathe too; then went back to fetch the gun.

"Stop!"

I looked up to see Leo, with the gun in his hand. He had slipped in quietly through the back way.

"Stop what?" I shouted resentfully.

But he was looking past me.

I snapped round to see Timmons was on his feet and staggering towards me, a knife in his hand. My left ear seemed to implode, then fell deaf as the gun cracked off beside me. Timmons crumpled to the ground, a few feet away; with two slugs in him. Leo paced past me, his expression unreadable- to me anyhow. Timmons was still alive, as he looked up at my brother, bleeding heavily from the wounds in his chest. Leo swiftly pressed the gun to Timmons's forehead and pulled the trigger.

Chapter 15

Leo swivelled round to look at me and the gun hung loosely at his side. I didn't know in that moment if he was a friend or an enemy, a brother, or stranger.

"I think you got him." I said squarely.

Leo exhaled slowly. He slipped the gun into his back pocket and plucked out a cigarette.

"There's a smoking ban you know," I said as he lit up.

He ignored me.

He looked down at the body and simply said, "Fuck."

We looked at each other, each trying to gauge the other. Each pretending we knew what to do or what was going to happen. Both failing to inspire any confidence- just like when we were stupid kids. I wiped at my head and covered it in a dusting of my own blood.

"Why did you have to get involved Jimmy?" he asked quietly, but with a hint of contempt in it.

"Why did you have to kill my best mate?" I countered,

"You're a fucking animal," I added, the anger bubbling over.

"What do you know about?" he spat, "He's the animal," he said and gave the cadaver a kick.

"Shite!" he shouted, pacing on the spot, sucking hard on his cig.

"Why d'ya do it? Just for the money- the fucking cash?

How did it start? 'Oh hello I see you're a psychopath, wanna work for me?'" I mocked.

"Something like that," he said with disinterest, just staring at the floor, thinking.

He began to pace about the room, as did I. His eyes followed my steps, studying me. It felt like a bull fight; the sparring at the beginning, the anticipation; but I didn't know who the matador was.

He breathed out hard again suddenly, "We had had a business arrangement going for a long time, lots of stuff. We were valuable to each other. I had a few guys lined up who could take the rap for things if needs be. Timmons was very useful to me. I'd spread a few rumours around every so often- bout a few lackeys just- who work for me. Timmons had a lot to lose and it wouldn't be good for me if he lost it- in any way. It wasn't until Davy Dick that he did a hit for me."

He stopped. He looked drained- old.

"You had Davy killed?"

"Yeah," he said simply, shrugging, "I saw something in him after that- a thirst. He wanted to do more- he liked it I suppose. He liked getting paid for it too, and it suited me."

112

"Suited you to kill everyone around you who caused you trouble? What about Stevie?"

He looked away.

"Stevie was a loose end. He knew too much- about the Davy stuff," he looked back at me, "Maybe he was a mistake, I don't know."

"Am I loose end too?" I said, pacing closer to him now.

"Shut up Jimmy, I need to think."

"Fuck yourself Leo," I said and we both stopped, facing one another, both faces like thunder.

Unexpectedly he reached into his back pocket and pulled out the gun. My eyes blazed and my body tensed. My brain was still flitting through what to do next, when he swivelled the gun in his hand and brought it crashing down on my head. Then everything slowly slipped away, trickling; like the blood running over my eyes, and there seemed to be no Jimmy left, just black.

Chapter 16

"I only like the green grapes. Fucking pips in 'em too."

"You ungrateful bastard," said Pav, leaning over my hospital bed and giving me a kiss, "You seem a bit better today."

She swiped the bag of red grapes away.

"Yeah, can't wait to get out of this bloody place," I said, struggling to loosen the starched sheets to sit up.

"Where's the wee woman," I asked, glancing to the door.

"I put her in an extra day of nursery."

I nodded, "I miss you love."

"You too," she said, and her eyes glistened, her face falling, "You need to look after yourself better."

"I know," I agreed, "Has there been anything on the news, my telly's on the blink again," I asked- nodding to my pay-as-you-watch set.

"No, nothing. It's still big news though. They think he's definitely skipped the country, but they don't know where."

I nodded again, I didn't know what to feel.

"It was the policeman's funeral today- Mr. Merritt," she added.

"Poor bugger," I said.

"It was big."

"I doubt there'll be many at Timmons's."

"No."

We both fell silent for a moment and Pav took my hand. I tried to take some kind of comfort that the worst must be over. But actually it wasn't.

...

Bongo Fury 3:
Dancing Madly Backwards

Chapter 1

"Fuck this shit."

"Sorry?"

"Pardon my French."

"Your French?"

"It's an expression love. Anyway, sorry for cursin'."

Pavla fixed me with a look and then I really was sorry.

"I'm sorry- seriously this time. I'm just being grumpy," I said.

We had been squabbling during breakfast, and in earshot of Skye.

"Come here you silly shit," she said quietly and hauled me towards her. That's no easy task considering my sizeable bulk, opposed to her tiny frame. Skye turned from CBeebies and gave us her own withering look as if to say, 'You two scunder me.'

"I'm sorry love," I said again, holding Pav tightly.

"It's okay Jimmy, I know you are."

As I drove off to the shop, something struck me as it had done many times before. I was a lucky git.

A jammy wee git.

Pavla is one in a million. It had been a two minute fight-beginning with something stupid about if Skye should be allowed any sugar on her cereal and ending with who's job was it to take the cat to the vet. Incidentally- that's a worse chore than you'd expect. Our cat, though technically a geriatric at fifteen years old, can fairly move when confronted with the vet. Aside from ending up with wrists like you've been arm wrestling Freddie Kruger, the stupid cat has you chasing it all over the place, much to the vet's unhidden annoyance. Anyway, the fact is that the argument was very trivial and I recognize that I'm a lucky bastard. Pavla's been very patient. It had been six months since Leo cracked me over the head, hospitalised me and did a runner. I hadn't felt quite the same afterwards. And Leo hadn't been seen since. As I sent the rusted and newly graffitied metal shutter crashing upwards, I surveyed Bongo Fury, my little slice of the earth. Once inside, I had time to switch on the music and brew a pot of coffee before opening up to the hoards of Bangor's music lovers. There was nobody there. That wasn't unusual. I would make one sale during a morning and be pleased with it. It didn't help that there was a new record shop that had opened up in the town. Maybe I had lost out on some customers already to them. Admittedly it was difficult to tell. Competition- good for everyone isn't it? Fuck that.

Chapter 2

My only visitor that morning was one Brian Caskey. Brian's from up the road in Belfast; a good guy, knows his music. He's ex-RUC and does some PI work himself too. He's a writer as well- crime fiction of course.

"'Bout you Brian, you're a bit early aren't you?"

"How's it going Jim, yeah well you could say that," he said, dramatically checking his watch, "But you are also just about the only place about to buy a record."

"Very true. Sales are always welcome. Cuppa mate?"

"Aye, I'd love one."

I brewed my third pot of the day and pulled us a couple of stools up behind the counter. Brian's a bit older than me, taller too, but probably half my weight. I'd been doing extra weights at the time and bulked up to nearly my biggest ever. Apart from the smoking and drinking, I was fit as a butcher's dog. There's a wee touch of white nipping at his temples, whereas my glorious locks have stayed jet black and full- so far anyway, thank fuck.

"Can you have a wee drink tonight, or are you driving?"

"'Fraid not, gotta be sensible tonight. Pav's at her class in the morning, so I'll be on breakfast and school run duty. It'll be a half six job."

"Sound painful."

"Aye, it does alright. I'll have a wee *J* or two anyhow. What about you?"

"Yeah, I fancy a few beers like. I might get a lift back with my publisher- she lives up in town, or I'll even get the train. Be nice to take the edge off."

Brian was releasing a collection of short stories and I had said he could launch it in the shop that night. He figured it'd be quirky. I'd been putting on a few events in the shop recently anyway- not usually book launches mind. A couple of local groups had done some acoustic sets. It brought a few more customers in- man's got to eat like. Speaking of which- it reminded me that I wanted to check out my competition later on.

"There's another reason I called in- you'll like this- random." He slurped the last of his coffee and set down the black mug that was emboldened with a Thin Lizzy logo.

"So, I get a phone call earlier on- guy says he wants a wee investigation job done. I tell him that I'm too busy. 'Cause Jim, with this new book coming out- I'll hopefully get a wee bit of interest and I've two jobs on at the minute already as it is. Anyway- then the guy asks if I know anyone else. And I say- 'aye I might do.' So I think of you Jim- are you interested?"

"Well, yeah I might be. Cheers. So, what kind of set up is it?"

"I don't have the detail yet- but he says it's just a bit of digging. But, there is something else- you'll get a kick out of it."

"Go on then," I say, hitting him a gentle shove.

"He tells me his name- David McKinty."

He smiled at me and I searched my at times *slow computing brain*. I'd get there.

"Not from Fugue?"

"I asked him that and he sounded a bit embarrassed. But aye it's him."

I laughed, "That's pretty cool. Jesus- I haven't heard much about him for years."

"Yeah- I think he left the music industry altogether. Just your man still plays- what you call him- the drummer..."

"Alan Devlin."

"Aye- he's got that other band going."

Fugue had been a pretty huge band from Belfast back in the late seventies/ early eighties. They were a kind of stoner blues rock outfit and they even fired a few singles into the charts that became minor hits. They had a loyal following. They'd have been like a slightly lesser known Boomtown Rats. Maybe if one of them had got rich rock stars to rattle a jar for charity they'd have been bigger. By the way Sir Bob- "No rain or rivers flow?" What about the Congo? Or the fucking Nile?"

"No way- weird! Well, yeah sure I'd be interested- will hear him out anyway. Cheers Brian."

Chapter 3

By the time we had another coffee and Brian headed on,
it was lunch time. I stuck a back in a half hour sign on the
door and drove into Bangor town centre, finding a space
up on High Street. You usually could as Bangor town
centre is post apocalypse these days. You'd be as likely
bumping into a zombie as finding a shop still in business. I
soon found my new rival- 'Bending Sound Records'.
Nicked my monopoly on vinyls and my first letter too. I
walked along towards it and looked up at the sign. I didn't
think much of the yellow. Roger Waters was on a poster in
the window too- another prick. "Alright?" said the guy
behind the desk as I sauntered in. It was the owner- I'd
seen him in the local paper after it opened. I never got a
picture in the paper when I started up back in the day. He
was around my age, brown hair with glasses. I gave him a
nod. There was one other person leafing through the stacks
of vinyl on shelves. He glanced round at me and I
recognised him as a regular of mine. I fixed him a look and
his face fell before he turned back round and busiest
himself with his search. I admit the inside of the store
looked good. Everything was neatly spaced out and
organised. It wasn't too cramped and there were some nice
new posters on the walls and a row of pricier records

running round, just below the ceiling. I approached the letter *A*. Good a place to start as any.

"Let me know if you need any help," the owner shouted across, looking over the rim of his glasses.

"Cheers," I replied gruffly.

Fucksake- gimme a chance to look like. This isn't Versache.

I began to leaf through them. Everything was in a shiny new plastic sleeve, there was some good stuff too. It was pissing me off. My soon to be ex-customer sheepishly paid for a record, before shuffling out and leaving us record sellers alone. I sauntered down to the end of the row.

"Have you heard the last Roger Waters?" asked the owner, suddenly, now at my back.

Jesus. He gave me a start.

I couldn't wait to get out of there.

"No mate, I'm more of a Gilmour man."

"I don't see the point in taking sides when it comes to music," he said with a wide smile. He paused, "You're the guy runs Bongo *whatyoucallit,* aren't you?"

"Bongo Fury," I corrected him, "It's after a Beefheart album. Better get back to it actually."

"Yes of course- more a Zappa release though wasn't it?"

I shrugged.

"I'm Steven by the way, I'm not long opened."

"Yeah, I know who you are," I said and left.

Chapter 4

I admit I was in a bit of a mood for the rest of the afternoon, but I snapped out of it once I got home. Skye was in super sweet form after nursery. We played *monsters* and then we cuddled up and watched the last hour of CBeebies. Pav had made us a delish veggie curry and a wee glass of red finished it off nicely. By the time I was kissing them both goodbye and was heading back down to the shop, I felt like myself again.

"Not a bad turn out Bri," I said patting him on the back. We had nipped out the back for a smoke. He had a roll up and I had something a little stronger. There were about thirty people crammed into my little shop. I'd run out of chairs- even the 'occasional' ones. The last few punters had to make do with a couple of vinyl flight cases stacked together.

"Yeah, it's dead on, cheers again for hosting. I owe you one."

"Not a problem mate."

"In fact- I can repay the debt pretty soon. Your man said he might call in tonight.

"Who- David McKinty?"

"Aye- he might show up, so we'll have to see what he has to say."

We went inside, charged our glasses and then I introduced Brian and said how pleased I was to launch his book, which was true. I also pointed out that I would give a generous ten percent off all records for one night only. *Stick that in your pipe 'Bending Sound'.*

"I want to read you the first story from the collection. It's not too long, so don't panic," said Brian. There was a little ripple of laughter. It looked like it helped to settle his nerves. "So, here we go... *'A Neighbourly Helping Hand. Dorothy eased into her summer chair and gently relaxed her body fully, letting out a small and satisfied sigh. She had worked in her garden all morning and was pleased with her progress. The roses had been pruned, the clematis clipped back and the hanging baskets tidied up. She surveyed her kingdom; a small corner plot in the sought after Cherryvalley, on the outskirts of Belfast. The calm and tranquillity was a far cry from the hustle and bustle of the now hiving city centre. She sipped her Earl Grey tea, brushing a few crumbs off her navy blouse, left by the indulgent lemon biscuit she had just consumed. She would be hitting seventy soon and had still managed to maintain a slender figure, but not without substantial will power. It was a mild May morning and the weather had been very kind of late, in a country where the weather could be as unforgiving as some of its warring tribes. A magpie flew over Dorothy's magnolias and landed on her next door neighbour's tiled roof. Then it fluttered abruptly away. She looked over towards the house and gave a small shudder. She could view part of her neighbour's front garden from her current vantage point and thankfully there was no sign of her. Sipping the last mouthful of tea, she set down the cup on its saucer on the freshly mowed grass and lifted up her new paperback. Having one last glance around the avenue, she was contented and cracked open the spine. It was the latest bestselling Scandi thriller and one that her conservative book club neighbours would not have approved of. She dived in and was at once immersed. A bleak landscape, a secret, a body, a hard living detective..*

"Dorothy!"
Clutching her chest, her heart reminded her of its age.

"Maureen, you startled me," she gasped, looking up, her neighbour towering over her. Maureen was around her age, a little less cared for in all ways. There was an arrogant scowl across her heavily bronzed face, a newly quaffed hair do dancing incongruously above it.
"Dorothy, I believe I just observed one of your cats crossing my lawn."

Her tone was somewhere between Miss Truchbull and Miss Havishham.

"Oh," said Dorothy, recovering from the start she had been given, "I'm sorry, did they relieve themselves in your garden?"

"No," she replied indignantly, as if fearing a trick, "But they were trespassing."

"Well, I'll have a word with them both Maureen," Dorothy replied flatly.

Maureen continued to stare with righteous anger, then turned on her heel and stormed away. Dorothy shook her head and lifted her paperback up again, but the peace had been ruined.

The next day, Dorothy was preparing a chicken and mango curry to be heated up later for guests that evening. The doorbell chimed its chipper ring and Dorothy clicked off radio four and hurried to the front door.

"Hello Dorothy," greeted Reverent Tom warmly.

"Tom, lovely to see you, please come in."

"I won't thanks, I just wanted to drop in the church newsletters..."

"...That is a turning circle!" boomed a voice abruptly from behind them.

Reverent Tom swivelled around and Dorothy searched past him, her stomach knotting. Maureen was stood, arms crossed, power dressed in what resembled a cloak above her blouse and skirt. She cocked her head to the side and looked between them and the minister's silver polo, parked just outside. Her head flicked back and forth, her quiff a little slow in following the movements of it.

"You cannot park in a turning circle," she continued, "And this is a private road."

"Oh, I'm sorry," started Tom and Dorothy squeezed his arm once for support, "I was just leaving."

Maureen gave no reaction other than to wrinkle her brow further. Tom pressed the booklets into Dorothy hands and uttered a hasty goodbye. Dorothy briskly thanked him and waved him off. Maureen remained as she had been, on sentry.

"We must retain standards, she declared pointedly, after he had driven away.

"Yes Maureen," agreed Dorothy wearily, stepping back into her doorway.

"Clergy stopping in the turning circle, it's like the last days of Rome."

She shut the door tight.

...

Clip clip. Clip clip.

What was that?

A few days had passed and Dorothy was just pulling into her drive way, back from a stock up at Marks and Sparks. It was early afternoon and after a light drizzle, the day had turned out fine. Switching off the engine, the clipping noise could be heard even more distinctly through the half open window. It appeared to be coming from her side garden. Silently, Dorothy pushed the car door to and crept around the side of her home. There, crouched down with her back to her was Maureen. She was hunched over Dorothy's sweet pea, clipping furiously at it, leaves and flowers scattering everywhere.

"Maureen, what are you doing?" Dorothy blurted out instinctively.

Maureen continued to cut. Only a hunch of the shoulders suggested she had heard her.

"Maureen, stop!" She said louder.

Maureen continued to cut.

Exasperated, Dorothy strode forwards and clutched her neighbour's arm.

"Get off me!" screamed Maureen, turning and pushing Dorothy away.

Her eyes bulged and a vein pulsed in between two kidney spots on her temple. In shock, Dorothy took a step back, both enraged and bemused.

Turning her back again, Maureen returned to her cutting.

"You've let this become overgrown," she grumbled with a tisk.

Dorothy circled around her and spoke to her from the side.

"Maureen, stop this, it is my garden," she tried, gently.
No reaction.

Maureen continued to cut.

"Maureen- please, will you stop?" she asked, her patience hanging in tatters, much like her hacked sweet pea.

Clip, clip.

Maureen continued to slash like a woman possessed, now very little left of the blooming flowers.

"Maureen stop!" Dorothy commanded finally.

"No!" wailed Maureen, spinning around with her clippers raised. She paused and then lunged out and sliced them across Dorothy's arm.

"Ahh!," Dorothy shrieked. "I warned you!" cried Maureen. Dorothy clutched her bleeding arm; it was superficial but very painful. "Look what you've done," she whispered, aghast. "I said I warned you," barked Maureen, brandishing the secateurs, a dark twinkle in her eye. Surprising herself as much as anyone, Dorothy formed a fist and launched a right hook suddenly into Maureen's face. It caught her perfectly with a satisfying crunch and she fell backwards, spilling the clippers. She got to her knees and placed a hand to her burning cheek, staggered. Dorothy rubbed her own painful knuckles, adrenaline pumping and bringing along with it a huge surge of pleasure. Maureen pulled herself up from her knees, now in a fury. "You shouldn't have done that," she stated coldly, a sour nastiness in her voice. Then she dived for the shears with purpose. Noting the risk, Dorothy lunged after her, pouncing down and wrestling for them. They writhed on the ground, both grunting and growling. There was a tangle of blouses and patterned scarves. Maureen took the upper hand and plunged the shears towards Dorothy's neck, stabbing forwards. She missed. Dorothy released an elbow into Maureen's face, making *contact with her nose, releasing a jet of blood. The daily dose of warfarin wouldn't help with the flow. Maureen responded with a gutsy head butt, crashing into Dorothy's own nose with a sickening crunch. The rich green grass beneath them was now splattered by two streaks of blood. Maureen leaped on her again, like a woman half her age, straddling Dorothy's legs and trying to slice at her with the blade. In a moment of clarity, Dorothy's self defence training from a few years previous kicked in and she managed to block the swipes and half wrench the tool from Maureen's grip. The result left the jaws open and one of Maureen's fingers precariously in between them. Dorothy took her chance and pulled the handles sharply down with both hands.*

Snap.

The best of the weather had long passed and most on the avenue had resigned themselves to a poor summer. Dorothy let herself into her neighbour's house and climbed the stairs. She knocked the bedroom door and entered.

"It's only me," she said, setting a newly baked wheaten bread down on the bedside table.

Both parties had wanted to only record the incident as a 'bad gardening accident,' and no one had suspected anything or argued with that. Maureen's odd behaviour was well known, but nobody could have guessed at what had transpired in Cherryvalley that sun kissed afternoon.

In addition to the surgery following Maureen's loss of one finger, she had been prescribed a number of medicines to keep her calm and 'even her out' as the young doctor had called it to Dorothy. Oddly, after years of aggression from her neighbour- both passive and otherwise, Dorothy had fallen into the role now of her primary carer. With no friends or family, this was a position not in demand.

"Now then, where were we?" Dorothy said briskly.

She checked her back pocket for the shears and closed the bedroom door behind her.'

There was a sincere round of applause and the punters had laughed in all the right places okay. I was chuffed for Brian. There was another reading, a signing and some interesting questions from the audience. After everyone had gone and I had snibbed the door, we popped out for another smoke. We were fine in our short sleeves, though now that the daylight had faded, a breeze had begun to pick up a little.

"Well, what did you reckon? I think it went well Bri."

"Yeah, cheers, I'm pleased. Most people bought a book too."

"Happy days. I'll have to give it a wee read myself."

"I think you've earned a free copy."

I smiled as I sucked contentedly on the joint. "Will you ever go back to writing about that other fella- Billy... Billy Chapman?"

"Aye, I might do. Writing about a different character for a change is refreshing. When you go back to them again after a while, you enjoy it more."

Chapter 5

Brian had arranged to meet a few others down in the town and one of them swung back round to pick him up again. I waved him off as he shuffled out with his half box of books. I locked up the back and had just flung the lights off when there was a rap on the window. I flicked on the porch light and pulled the front door open. There was a man in his late sixties with a black duffel coat wrapped around him and grey trousers. His face looked spongy, rather than very wrinkled, and he had a distinctive hook nose.

Older, grayer, but it was David McKinty.

"David, come on in."

He looked pleased that I knew who he was.

"You must be Jimmy, nice to meet you," he shook my hand. It had a surprising tightness for a man of his age. I led him in and switched the lights back on.

"Can I get you something David- a wee coffee?"

He eyed the open half bottles of wine left on the counter.

"Could I get one of those?"

"Yeah, course you can, here, take a seat."

We got sorted with a glass each and I pulled up a couple of chairs from the back row. I hadn't bothered tidying anything and was leaving it till the morning.

"Thanks for that," he said, savoring a mouthful of red, "Good of you to see me too."

"Not a problem, I'm intrigued," I said, taking a sip myself, "I'm sure you hear it all the time but I really rated Fugue. I was a fan."

"Thank you," he said, tilting his head.

"Yous were just doing big things when I was in my formative years you could say. And then yous broke up before I got to see you play live- I was gutted."

"Well, apologies," he replied with a throaty chuckle, "Those were *challenging* times in many ways", he added with a knowing smile.

"So, what can I do for you?"

"Well," he said setting his glass down and unbuttoning his coat, "Maybe it's not too late to see us play live after all."

He gave me a look, two faded blue eyes twinkling at me.

"Oh?"

He went on to explain that he was hopeful that it might become a reality- even after being broken up for nearly thirty years. There was a determination in his eyes when he told me that it would be a dream to reunite with his old band mates again.

"And there would be financial benefits of course too," he added with another scratchy chuckle.

"Alan is up for it, but Ricky of course, is the unknown quantity."

"Ahh," I said, the penny dropping on what he might want.

Ricky Randall had been the outrageous longhaired singer/guitarist of the band. When they split up, he just disappeared. There were rumours that the music industry ground him down and he was just done with it. That he started a new life. The weird thing is- he really did just vanish. In Absentia. His parents were already dead and he wasn't married. His friends all said he went AWOL. Seemingly nobody had heard from him since, or didn't admit to it anyway. And several journalists had certainly tried to unravel the mystery. He was the local Lord Lucan for a time. There were the usual rumours like with Syd Barrett, Peter Green and the like. One random, but prevailing theory was that he had in fact retrained, moved to England and become a top anesthetist. Weird.

"So. That's the bottom line really, I want to pay you to see if you can find him for me. Or at least to find out what you can. What do you think?"

I clinked his glass.

"Why not?" I said.

"One other thing, Jimmy- I'd prefer you keep my name out of when you're asking around."

"Not a problem."

I was glad to have a wee case to work on- and this seemed like a cracker. But it was strange to be tasked with tracking somebody down. I should have been out there finding my own brother.

Chapter 6

Before bed, I went up to the roof space and enjoyed a
couple of J's. Maybe *enjoyed* is too strong. My head was
fried. I wasn't chilled out enough. The weed didn't
manage to relax me either. I was swimming with the buzz
of the event followed by this strange meeting with an old
guy that I used to listen to all the time when I was a
teenager. I put on Fugue's second album and cranked it up.
Life is so strange. That's what it's called- *Life is so
Strange.* The record spun and the needle gave out a
diminutive crackle of anticipation. Heavy seventies toms
gave way to overdriven bass and sweeping flangey guitar.
Where would I start trying to track him down? What right
did I have to try if he didn't want to be found? God knows
where I'd begin. David had said there was no point in
trying Alan as he hadn't heard anything of him since the
seventies. That would have been the obvious place. The
next spliff went down better and I lifted out a tin of
Heineken from my mini fridge to wash it down. I kept
thinking about Leo. I was so furious with the fucker- not
least so for putting me in the hospital and almost into a
comma. I was getting a little buzz on which was at odds
with thinking about Leo. I tried to push those thoughts to
the side and get into the music. It wasn't doing it for me, I

don't know why. I used to love it. Maybe it was just the easy going swagger of the songs jarring with my mood. The cops had come to see me a few days before and applied the usual bit of pressure to see if I'd heard from Leo. It went the same way as usual with them no better off and me unsure if they believed me. For fucksake- I had sold out my own brother already to find a rat in *their* force. It hadn't earned me any good grace anywhere.

I stubbed out my smoke and pulled the record off. I stared at my shelves for something that would suit my mood better. I wanted something to smoke a last spliff to. I made my selection and layered, droney guitar rumbled out of the speakers.

Black gives way to blue.

It's the 'come back' album Alice in Chains made after Layne Staley had died. It sounds good, blasting into my ears as I rolled up a last number. Not every fan is a fan of the new stuff- but I think it's great. They managed to carry on with another front man. Not every band can and maybe shouldn't. Fugue weren't able to. The side finished and the needle dropped to the side as the turntable automatically clicked off. I lay back and enjoyed the last puffs of my joint. Silence. The early Alice in Chains song *Brother* floated through my head,

"Frozen in the place I hide
Not afraid to paint my sky
With some who say I've lost my mind
Brother try and hope to find."

Chapter 7

The shop was quiet the next day. Not an original occurance. I spent the time wisely and began the search for my quarry. First off I used the amateur PI's best friends- Google and Wikipedia. There wasn't a great deal that was new to me or a surprise. I leaned over the counter, flicking through the various open pages on my laptop, sipping at a fresh cup of coffee. Ricky Randall was from a working class North Belfast family, the same as the other two guys. They had met at school and the band was signed by the time they were all twenty one. They had a quick rise, achieving a loyal following and decent sales. There were the usual tabloid stories of excess and all the rest of it and then it was all over. David had told me that Ricky couldn't handle the pressure any longer and called it quits, stunning the other two. After that, where he went was anyone's guess. He wasn't a top tier celebrity and there were plenty of other rock stars about the place, so nobody looked for him all that hard. Lots of folk had claimed to have met him over the years, but which stories were true were anyone's guess. With another pot brewing, I placed a few calls. I tried a guy I know in public records, one in the police and a girl who worked for The Belfast News. I didn't find out much else. It was like there was nothing to discover. But there had to be.

Abruptly my attention was drawn by the sharp ring from the bell over the shop door. Two fellas in their late twenties/ early thirties swaggered in. They both had on short sleeve shirts and wore jeans. Both sported multiple tattoos and exuded an unlikeable cockiness.

"Gents," I said evenly, straightening up, my back clicking. I folded over the laptop. I knew who these pricks would be.

"Jimmy," nodded the first one, looking pleased about something. He had bleached yellow hair and a shadow of a goatee. His ginger counterpart said nothing, spending all his brain power on trying to look tough.

"Are you two from the ukulele club by any chance?" I asked with a broad smile, "I've a lovely new selection out the back."

I stared from one to the other. Bleach sneered. Ginger looked confused.

"So, let's cut the crap, you know who I'm sent from," began Bleach, deciding to pitch it tough, "And you know it's about your brother.

"Do I indeed?"

"Aye, you do," he said, rolling his shoulders and strutting into the middle of the room. Ginger followed. Since the whole debacle with my brother, the leadership of the group had switched about some. It was like Game of Thrones, but with no dragons, only tits.

I slapped on my best bored face and shrugged.

"We need to know what your brother's at. You shouldn't mess around if you know. So have you heard from him or not?" he barked. He sounded more terrier than terrifying.

I took a step forward. This little prick was getting on my nerves now. The bored face had dropped off.

"I don't see what my relationship with my brother has to do with you, ya wee shitebag."

Ginger took a step forward.

"You stay where you are Prince Harry."

"This is a bit of a museum piece," he sneered, making a point of looking over the shop, "Be a shame still if something happened to it. Where'd you get all this junk from anyway?" he said, pointing at the vinyl section.

"Every time I fucked your mum, she bought me a record."

He looked ready to pop and his face turned as red as his mate's hair.

"Anyway, enough about your Ma. I'm the one who fuckin' worked out what was going on and told your bosses about it! And my brother cracked my head over it. I don't owe them nothin'."

"Your brother was killin' his way round town. He was targeting the organisation. Maybe you're covering for him now Jimmy."

I don't know what irked me more- the stupidly of his statement or the fact that he kept using my first name.

"Look, we don't wanna have to get rough here…"

Whack!

That had been all I needed to hear. I landed a full right into his jaw. He near hit the deck.

"Threaten me in my own shop will ya?" I hollered, steadying him, then grabbing his arm and twisting it behind his back. He cried out. Blood ran down off his face.

Ginger helplessly bobbed from one heal to the other.

"Stay put you," I spat at him, while twisting Bleach's arm higher, causing another whimper. Ginger looked like rigor mortis had already set in.

Bleach looked set to pass out so I eased off the pressure, then kicked him onto the ground. Ginger knelt down to help his buddy up. Colour began to return to his whitened face. They both stood.

"You shouldn't have done that," Bleach whispered hoarsely, "You're in some fuckin' trouble now…"

Thud.

That was the noise he made when he hit the dirt after I smacked him a second time. This time he did go out cold.

"Wake him the fuck up and get out of my shop."

Ginger did as he was asked. I leaned against the counter and slugged down the rest of my coffee. The bell made an incongruous high pitched rattle as they left.

Fuck.

I spent the rest of the day switching between rage and worrying about repercussions. Maybe I had gone too far. A few joints helped me to finally get off to sleep that night.

Then I woke up the next morning to discover that Bongo Fury had been burned to the ground.

Chapter 8

The call had come from the local police. I was speechless. I didn't see it coming at all.

"Pav…" was all I managed to shout, after I had mumbled my way to the end of the call.

"Jimmy, what is it?" She came running, her beautiful face was creased by worry, she instinctively knew it was bad.

I told her and we hugged. Thankfully Skye was already away to playgroup and didn't see me shed a tear or two. Life had given me one too many kicks recently.

"Thanks love," I said gratefully as Pav handed me a coffee with a brandy chaser and we sat down together on the sofa.

"Jimmy, tell me again all that the police man say."

I went through it again. They said that it had all but burned down and that they suspected arson. They said I could go and see it and asked if I could come to the station at midday to make a statement.

"I'm so sorry Jimmy. It'll be okay. We're insured, we can start again."

I nodded non-comitally. I busy thinking through who could have done this. And the fury was rising slowly but surely.

Driving to the shop, I concluded that there was only really one suspect. I had gone through anyone I had had a disagreement with (which wasn't the shortest of lists) but nobody jumped out at me. I didn't figure it was Leo and I doubted it was a bent copper getting back at me for all that had happened. My new record shop rival? Hardly, it must have been a short, sharp reaction to me roughing up those two goons. Whoever had actually carried it out- the order had come from the new top guy- Mike Kinney.

I felt drawn to see it. It was like needing to see a loved one in their casket. Though my beloved shop had already been cremated. There was a cordon around it when I parked a little way up the hill. There was still one police car and one fire truck outside. I got slowly out of the car and shuffled towards it in disbelief. Smouldering crates of records had been dumped out onto the street and the blackened front shutter was lying beside them. The sign up above was just about hanging on, but it was scorched and hard to read. I turned on my heel and returned to my car.

Chapter 9

I spent the minimum time I could down at the cop shop. I'm not sure what they were glaring about, but they *were* glaring. It could have been they thought I was on an insurance dodge and did it myself. It could have been because I had taken down one of their own when they hadn't noticed he was bent. Or maybe they didn't care for my Fugazi T-shirt or my manners. Fuck knows. To paraphrase Chandler, I don't care much for my manners either and I grieve for them over a spliff nightly.

"Any more ideas who did it Jimmy?" Pav asked as we shared a bottle of wine with our dinner. I had only talked about my thoughts on that more generally with her so far. I forked some bolognaise into my mouth and watched Skye struggling with her spaghetti, her brow furrowed. I let a smile creep across my lips. At least nobody had been harmed in the blaze.

"Well, it's like I said earlier- these guys- the connected ones- they don't like what Leo did. They don't like that I was involved with it, that I was the one figured it out. Hell, the cops don't like that much either. Fucked if I didn't piss off everyone, trying to get at the truth. Sorry," I said, lowering my voice, looking at Skye. Maybe we should just leave this shithole place."

"Language Jimmy," she said, her brow lowering into a furrow.

"Sorry love," I said raising a hand and glancing at Skye again as she obliviously toiled on with her dinner.

"They sent two goons to see me a few days ago," I admitted quietly.

"What? What about? Jimmy you have to tell me these things."

"I know, I know, I'm sorry."

She wasn't angry. But she was scared and gripped my hand hard.

"They come and ask every so often- ask where Leo is."

"Well you don't know that," then her expression faltered, "Do you Jimmy?"

"No, of course not Pav, frigsake."

"I'm sorry. What happened?"

I twisted in my chair, "Well, it got a little heated."

"Jimmy," she scolded.

"It wasn't my fault. I didn't invite it."

"I know, I know Jim," she said, indicating for us both to keep calm. Skye looked up and we both smiled back at her, pretending everything was all gravy.

"Keep going wee love, it's yum," I said to her.

"We'll get through this," Pav said leaning over and kissing my cheek.

I felt guilty. Guilty because my family was being impacted by this shit. And guilty too because I knew exactly where my brother was.

Chapter 10

The next morning I went out, under the guise of sorting insurance stuff all day. I did do some of that, but I also just needed a distraction. I decided I'd work on the Fugue thing. I headed up to Belfast, then dandered around the city centre in a daze. I ate a McDonalds, smoked a joint and nodded respectfully to the burnt out Primark building as I passed by. Maybe some of those billionaires saving Notre Dame could spare a penny or two for Primark and Bongo Fury. I called in on my friend Natalie from The Belfast News. She had a half hour to spare and brought me in for a coffee and catch up. I got the chance to question her some more.

"I'm so sorry about your shop Jim," she said, her face looking pained. She gave me a hug, her purple hair trailing down my back. She's a good girl is Natalie. She's someone who wears every feeling on her face.

"Thanks, it is shit, like. Unfortunately there's no point in investigating that one."

"You know who it was?"

"Yeah, I reckon so, but I can't touch 'em."

"That's Northern Ireland for you."

I shrugged.

We chatted some more, then she dug out her notebook about a story she had started on Ricky Randall a while back. She had hit dead ends almost everywhere she had looked. She had followed some streams for a few months that had gone absolutely nowhere.

Ricky had changed his name and married a fan.
Ricky had overdosed, died and it had been all hushed up.
Ricky was living in a cave. Etc. etc.

One rumour she had followed up on was the one about Ricky ending up working in a hospital in England. She had a name and address, but no proof. I thanked her and was on my way again. David had said there would be no point in going to see Alan Devlin, the ex Fugue drummer. I thought I may as well though. There weren't many open avenues to choose from. He ran a music collective on the edge of town. They had a music studio and band support and even their own mini label. When I got there a drizzle was starting and I didn't spend long taking in the warehousey exterior. I pressed the intercom and after a crackle, a muffled voice answered. It sounded like a young girl. We couldn't hear each other very well, but she buzzed me in anyway. I entered into a dimly lit hallway. There was some kind of office off to the left, but it was in darkness. I could hear muffled voices speaking upstairs, but most prominently was the sound of a band rehearsing up ahead. I walked on to the double doors and swung them open. Music poured out towards me. I stepped inside to three sets of eyes all on me. But they kept doing what they were doing, not missing a beat. The room would probably have held a few hundred, but there were only the three men playing on the small stage in front of me. They were covering a Stones song. It was a good version. The two men at the front were younger than me and much younger than the man seated behind them: Alan Devlin.

They finished the number before he said "take a break," to the other two. This must be the comically named 'Baking Powder Pigeons', Devlin's current band. He hopped down off the stage, as agile as a much younger man. His hair was full and black, but I guessed nature had had some assistance with it.

"Can I help?"

His voice was authoritative, but not aggressive.

"Good to meet you," I said, offering my hand, "The name's Black, Jimmy Black," I said in my best Bond.

I gave him a quick explanation of what I had been doing and he brought me over to the side where there was a bar.

"Well, I don't think I'll be much help to you. Jesus- that was all nearly forty years ago. But sure, have a wee dram while we have a chat anyway. Whaddya fancy?"

"Cheers, a pint of stout would do great, thanks."

We sat down at a table in the corner, while the bassist and guitarist sat up at the bar together.

"So, where do you think Ricky went to?" I asked him directly.

He blew out his cheeks, then took a sip of his half of bitter.

"God only knows. Seriously, anything is possible."

He flashed me a warm smile and his eyes were bright, "You know... Ricky was quite the character. I mean- he got himself into all kinds of scrapes."

"Drugs? Women?"

"Oh yeah, amongst other things. Look, he was always going to implode. Fuck knows what went on with him. He was always getting himself in shit. I just hope he ended up sorting himself out."

"So you've no ideas?"

"I'm sorry, no bloody clue."

We sipped at our drinks.

"Here's another question before I leave. If he turned up now, would you ever get Fugue back on stage?"

I thought he was going to choke on his pint laughing.

"I'll think about it- if you track Ricky down!" he said with a wry smile. I haven't even talked to David for years."

"You haven't seen him?"

"No, not for years."

"Oh," I said simply.

Chapter 11

That evening, I went for a walk after dinner. I needed to get milk and bread from the shop anyway. Things at home had been as normal as they could be, we tried extra hard for Skye's sake. As I turned left at the bottom of the street, I was conscious of a car slowing beside me. The hair on my neck prickled. I turned. It was a black Audi. Mike Kinney was seated in the passenger seat, beside a burly driver. His slicked back, graying hair sat obediently above his smug expression. His piss hole eyes bore into me. The car slowed to what must have been five miles an hour. I stopped dead, stared back at him and raised my arm. Then I raised my middle finger. His grim smile faltered. Not the reaction he had wanted I imagined. I held that stance until to the car had disappeared away into the distance.

The next few days were uneventful. I struggled with trying to work out what to do about Kinney and his cronies. My best option appeared to be to do nothing. I met Brian for a pint and that helped. It was good to talk about it all with a mate. His opinion was the same, that there was nothing for me to do. Hopefully they would think we were square now, even if I didn't.

I spent much of the next days enjoying lots of quality time with my girls and that was really nice. Then one afternoon, Natalie phoned me with an update. "Jimmy, I was looking through my stuff again- all the leads and tip offs to me and to other journalists that I've shared stuff with."

"Okay."

"There's not many of them that support one another. But that one about working in a hospital, it comes from three different sources. There's some credibility linked to the sources, we've got levels of judging for evaluating these things. Anyway, I just thought you'd want to know. It's certainly the strongest lead we have."

We chatted for a few more minutes. I felt excited. She also said that for one of the sources linked to it, there was just a basic email address and it was coupled to a bogus Google account. She knew a guy that had the knowhow and might spend a bit of time working through the chain, possibly getting back to a real name. I came off the phone buzzing. It was nice to have something to focus on. That and my girls. They had been brilliant. They kept me grounded, kept me from cracking the fuck up over everything; Leo, all the shit with the hoodrats, the shop. That night I had a couple of glasses of wine with Pav, binged a few episodes on Netflix. After she went to bed, I had a few rockets upstairs and banged on Entroducing by DJ Shadow. I hadn't listened to it for fucking years. Great stuff. I went to bed feeling better than I had done for a long while.

Chapter 12

Pav and me had a breakfast in the local greasy spoon the next morning after dropping Skye off. We both had a full Ulster and shared a plate of chips on the side. It was lethal! Afterwards, Pav went grocery shopping and I went to sort more Bongo Fury stuff. I really wasn't sure what I was going to do once the insurance and everything was sorted. One step at a time. On the way to my car, my phone went.

"Alright Jimmy, just wanted to see how things are going."

It was David. I told him about the shop.

"Shit, that's terrible, I'm sorry to hear that, what a sickener."

He was either savvy or discreet enough not to ask if I suspected who might have done it or why. We chatted on. I told him who I had spoken to and said that I had a few leads I was checking out. He seemed happy enough.

"While you're on David, you said you were alright to cover expenses, right?"

…

Pav took a bit of convincing, but two days later and I was on a ferry bound for Liverpool. I had a name and address and a little bit of hope. Looking back, I was probably close to a fucking nervous breakdown. Sometimes throwing yourself into something is the only way forward, for me anyway. I just needed space from all the crap. I was too up and down. Maybe Pav saw that. She didn't give off to me about it, she was great. I felt positive about the whole thing. But as I drove down off the car ramp, a downpour burst from the sky. I flicked the wipers onto the 'wipe like fuck' setting. The city beyond looked sprawling and I had a brief wobble on what the hell I was doing there. I whacked on Google Maps and put my head down. I was totally stuck in evening rush hour traffic. In a way it made it easier because it was nice and slow for me to follow the route without stressing out. It gave me the chance to look around too. The buildings were impressive and the place was bustling, it already felt good to be somewhere different. After about a half hour I was parked up in my basic-but-clean chain hotel. I threw a few things out on the chair in the corner and left my suitcase on the bed. The rain had passed and it was mild, so I headed out, just in a T-shirt, with a flannel shirt over the top. The evening sun had come out, placing a warm glow onto the wet streets. I savoured the smell of damp petrol and headed out to explore the city. As I glanced in a sports shop front window plastered with at least four Liverpool strips, my phone buzzed again. Part of me missed the peace and disconnectedness before the bloody things. "Hello." "Jimmy."

I didn't recognize the voice, but knew the type of prick it would be.

"Who's this?"

"Are you ready to talk about Leo yet? Just an address would do."

"Is this a cold call? No I don't want to change my broadband and you can shove PPI up your hole."

"It was a shame about the fire Jimmy."

"It would be a shame if my fuckin' boot went up your ass!"

I shouted and hung up. I was seething. I had a brisk walk up and down a few cobbled side streets to calm down. I would have loved a joint. Instead I called into a corner shop and bought a packet of fags and smoked a few one after another. I rang Pav for a chat and calmed down soon enough. Soon I was seated in a pub booth by myself, with a half drunk pint of stout and a plate of chips. I felt better again. Natalie had sent me a file with all of the research on Ricky Randall. I was chuffed with myself that I had managed somehow to extract it all and save it to the

Kindle app on my phone. A modern man! I sat, dipping chips in ketchup and learning a bit more about my quarry. I was starting to think that he had been a bit of a shit. The public image had been that of a *Cheeky Belfast Rocker*. She had scanned in a few articles from the time where he seemed a bit more of a hell raiser and womanizer than I'd realised. There were several groupies complaining about being picked up and dropped by him all in an evening. Then there were a few of the unsubstantiated claims that accused him of inappropriateness, or even rape. These weren't supported any better than the ones about him living in a cave with long fingernails. So, who knows. Still, no smoke without fire. I put my phone away, finished my chips and went off in search of The Cavern.

Chapter 13

I was up early, bought an over priced breakfast at the hotel, then hit the road. I had found the Cavern the previous night and had enjoyed another few pints inside. In the morning I felt the stirrings of a hangover, just round the edges. The fry had helped, even if potato and soda breads were absent. The English can't do a proper fry.

Fed and watered, I pulled off onto the motorway, my destination was Wigan- about a forty minute drive away. I whacked on some *Old School Chilis* and funked out, sitting mostly at eighty, wondering all the way if this was actually going to be him. I also tried to block out any of the more serious stuff from back home, that I should have been focused on. Anyway, I did have a job to do. Maybe this would be the mystery solved. Had this rock n roll cliché ended up secretly as a respected and sensible anesthetist? Fuck knew.

"Yes hello, Derek Caldwell please."

The receptionist disappeared into the room behind.

Derek? Surely he couldn't have become a 'Derek'. She returned again after making a call. Following a brief chat and my saying that I just needed a few minutes and that I had come all the way from Belfast, she disappeared once more. This time on her return she asked me to, "Please come this way."

Result.

I was left into a small, lime coloured office. There was a little desk with a PC on it and a seat behind it. There was a half size book shelf beside those, and I was seated in front of it all- almost within the swing of the door. I knew this whenever the door swung open and a middle aged, very tall man, strode in. I stood, surveying him closely as he whipped past me and moved behind the desk. He was very tall- too tall? Of course the face looked different also- it was lined, forty years older and spectacled.

Could be him.

"Mr Black, you don't have an appointment…"

"Yes, I'm sorry," I said, interrupting him, "I won't take long."

The annoyance in his face grew. His voice had contained irritation too and the unmistakable twang of a not altogether lost Ulster accent.

He gestured reluctantly for me to sit and folded his long legs into his own chair.

"Okay, what is this all about?"

Suddenly I felt very foolish.

What the fuck could I say?

I usually have jibber for any occasion, but I couldn't think how the hell to phrase this one.

"I… I've come across from, well *our country*."

He winced.

"I… em… investigate things sometimes. I was given some information…"

"For God's sake," he guldered, standing up abruptly, "Is this more of the Ricky Randall nonsense again? Good grief- what is it with you people?"

I stood as well, trying to keep neutral body language. If this jumped up wee berk got any antsier, I'd have to resist planting him one.

"So you're denying being Ricky Randall?"

"Of course I am! I'm five years younger than him for a start. I didn't live across the water until I went to university, which would have happened to be around the time he disappeared. But obviously I hadn't up till then been leading a double life of part time school boy, part time *Rock Star*."

I shuffled where I stood, "Can you prove any of that?"

He groaned and rolled his eyes before hurrying over to the computer and loudly punching at the keys. I watched as he hit a few more buttons, then he scrolled down carefully with the mouse.

"There you are," he declared, swinging the monitor around to face me, "My official HR account and here's their scan of my birth certificate."

I took my time reading through it, searching for something that didn't seem genuine. Then I took some more time, I'd come along way after all.

"Well?" he asked impatiently, "I really need to get on."

"Thanks for your time Mr Randall," I said before leaving.

I knew he wasn't Randall, as I hurried out of the building. I just wanted to piss off that self important wee twat.

I wondered around aimlessly, when I was back in Liverpool in the afternoon. Things felt a bit flat. I saw a few of the sites, called into The Beatles museum. I got me and Pav matching mugs and a pink Beatles T-shirt for Skye. I was sitting in a coffee shop with a door stop of coffee cake when a call came through from Natalie.

"My guy traced some of those user names."

"Okay. Great."

"He got a positive on one of the tips about your man in England."

I would have been more interested a few hours ago, I thought to myself.

"Same guy was also behind more of the tips, using different accounts."

"Tell me."

"It was David McKinty."

"Shit."

"Yeah- is that a surprise then?"

"Yeah it is."

"That's the bass player from Fugue, right?"

My heart was racing, mouth dry, "Yeah it is."

"You wanna tell me who your client is?"

"Nope. I can't yet, I'm sorry love. But if there's a scoop- you know it'll be yours. And I owe you many pints."

"Yeah you do," she said, before hanging up.

What the fuck?

First off he lies to me about trying to get the band together with Alan. Now he's been dropping anonymous tips, but keeping it from the guy he pays to investigate it. *What the hell is he playing at?*

Chapter 14

The whole Ricky Randall thing had been a welcome
distraction. Also, it was a bit of a melt. It had certainly
contained more twists than I had expected. But I was
toying with myself. I had been using it to look the other
way. And it had offered me an opportunity. It was like
pretending to yourself you'd take a spell off the drink
while bunging a six pack into the cooler. You already
know what's going to happen. That's the way I had been
on this trip, even when I first planned it. Like I said earlier,
I had known where my brother was hiding out for
sometime. He was in Leeds. My ferry home was due to
leave first thing in the morning. Plenty of time. I hit the
road. Google Maps had originally predicted me a journey
of under an hour and a half. Hitting the tail end of rush
hour added the guts of another hour. I was in the mood for
some rock to keep me going both mentally and physically.
I cracked through the back catalogue of the Seventies
stoner rock band- Captain Beyond. That and three or four
coffee stops kept the wheels spinning. When I was
informed that my "destination is on the left", it was around
eight. I didn't know Leeds at all, but I didn't need to, to
tell the area was a shithole. I parked on a derelict piece of
land up the road, next to a large dumpster. I eyeballed a

group of teenagers on BMX's as they sped past, giving a little too much attention to my motor. I was on the outskirts of the city, in an estate with some high rises in the background and a warren of terraces and bungalows where I was. According to my information, Leo was hiding out in the bungalow on this particular street- in number thirty five. I trusted the source and apparently some local hoods who were connected to some of Leo's previously dealings were looking out for him over here. For a small fee, I'm sure. That was another thing- Leo had lifted all of the savings before he left, leaving his family back home borderline penniless. Who was keeping a roof over their heads? Yeah- Muggins here.

After getting out, I checked the car door a few times and cast a suspicious look up towards where the teenagers had disappeared. I straightened my shirt flat. My heart was racing. I slipped a hand inside my coat pocket. The kitchen knife I had bought earlier was safely hidden there.

Chapter 15

Okay, let's do this.

I didn't blink as I approached the small house. My eyes bore ahead. The blinds were all shut. There was no car out the front, just a few pieces of rubbish scattered around the garden. The old peeling gate creaked as I opened it. I marched straight to the door and knocked it twice. I heard an internal door open and footsteps approach. There was no glass or peephole in the door. A lock clicked and it swung back. And there he was.

"Hello Leo."

His face contorted into panic, but he swiftly controlled himself and returned to the grey and hollowed out weariness.

"I suppose you better come in," he said evenly.

He held the door and I walked past him and into the little living room. It was a bit of a dive and stunk of cigarette smoke and stale Chinese take away. It smelt like it hadn't been aired since the war- or cleaned. The door shut behind and he walked in and stood beside me. The skin on his face hung around the jowls. He had lost a lot of weight. He looked sallow, unkempt. He was dressed in an old track suit, the sharp suits a distant memory.

"How did you find me Jimmy?"

"That doesn't really matter does it? It looks like you're doing well," I said ironically, gesturing to the room.

He clicked his tongue. He kept his arms at his sides, taught.

"You can sit down if you want, but I need to pat you down first."

I breathed out dramatically, "I'll save you the trouble," I said, reaching into my inside pocket. His eyes widened as I started to pull out the knife. Then he lunged at me- pushing me backwards, shoving me hard in the chest. I spilled the knife and fell sharply against a chair. He followed up with two jabs to my face.

Fucksake.

Now I was pissed.

I took the punches- they stung a wee bit- then I ducked his next swing. I came underneath and punched him hard near the elbow, almost breaking his arm. He yelled. I took a step back, took my time, then launched a brutal volley of punches to his face. His guard was nowhere. Blood pissed from his nose and he fell backwards and ungraciously into the sofa. I picked up the knife and stepped around the sofa to stand over him. He clutched his nose. There was no fight left in him. Pathetic.

"I brought this to show you what I could have done," I said brandishing the knife. I slipped it back in my pocket.

"You remember that. I was always stronger than you, you piece of shit. You're lucky you stayed down 'cause I would've enjoyed playin' with you a little more. You did put me in the hospital after all. Only 'cause you had a shooter, mind."

He pulled a tissue out of his pocket and began mopping up the blood from his face, "What'dya want- gratitude?"

"I could have stabbed you. But I'm not like you. You've many people's blood on your hands. But you're not the big *I am* anymore are you? And not a friend to be seen for it all- look at this shithole."

"I'm doing fine," he muttered, convincing nobody.

"Aye. And I want you to know this is us done. I don't wanna see you again, that's it. A lot of people have it in for you- but I'm not gonna give you to them. Fair warning- I might have to give them this address- so you might wanna move on."

"What the fuck?" he said irately, reaching for his cigarettes off the table.

"I might need to give them something." I sighed, "They burnt down my shop."

"Shit," he said, sounding like there was some genuine surprise and sympathy.

"Yeah." I fixed him a look in his eye, "Because I wouldn't give you up."

He was about to say something, then stopped.

"I'm sorry about that Jim." He resisted my stare. His eyes looked filled with sadness. I imagined much of it was for himself.

"Anyhow, that's how things stand," I said turning.

He stood up, squinting as he took in quick draws from the newly lit cigarette. He didn't seem bothered when ash fell onto the ancient carpet. I stopped. He looked like he was going to say something, but didn't. I moved on into the hallway and walked slowly back towards the front door. My stomach was churning. I turned. I saw tears in his eyes and he looked once more like he wanted to say something. I waited. He nodded to me. I turned and pulled the handle and headed out the door.

Chapter 16

I didn't sleep well that night. I had a few jars to help me along, but they didn't really help. There was a cold slab of sadness resting on my chest. I was restless all night, sweating, in and out of murky dreams. I departed Liverpool the next morning on a low. I took comfort in the fact that I had done right by him. But it was all too raw to feel anything but a great heaviness.

On board, I sat in the bar, leafing absently through a daily paper. Through the window I could see the fresh wake left as we cut through the choppy morning waves. I rang Pav and got speaking to Skye too, which cheered me a little.

I allowed myself just the one drink. They didn't have any stout, so I supped at a pint of bitter. I flipped out my phone and figured I'd pass the time by looking again through some of the material from Natalie. What was David playing at? After scrolling back and forth through the documents for about an hour, I thought I might have found something. I ordered a coffee and went through the page again. It was about the woman who had emailed Natalie and claimed to have been raped by Ricky Randall when she was fifteen.

Fuck.

A couple of Google searches confirmed it.

Fuck. Fuck. Fuck.

She was David McKinty's sister.

Chapter 17

I had texted David to say I needed to meet. I wanted to
see my girls first really but I also needed to speak with him
about it all. I thought once I did that- I could concentrate
on them. He agreed to meet with me late afternoon.
Driving back off the ferry through Belfast, my mind
worked overtime on just what the fuck David was doing.
Presumably he knew about what his sister was accusing
his former band mate of? How long had he known about it
for? Maybe she had only recently wanted to speak about it,
maybe after the whole #MeToo thing. But why had he
gone to great lengths to provide a tip off while covering
his identity? Why? And he had lied about seeing Alan and
wanting to get the band back together. It seemed to me the
reason must be that he wanted Randall found, but it not to
be connected to him. Why? Maybe I was the means to an
end and the end was David getting his hands on Ricky
Randall. My head was busted.

I had asked him to meet me at Bongo Fury. Or what was
left of it. I parked up and got out and smoked a cigarette. I
promised myself I wouldn't form a habit of it. The spliffs
were a bad enough habit as it was. I drew in deeply, hardly
able to wait until I had a joint down my neck. I sniffed my
fingertips, they stunk of smoke- then I walked up to my

old shop. My fingers were nothing compared to the stale and overpowering stench coming from the shop. The front door was somehow still in place, even though the window beside it was now filled with cardboard. Surprisingly, my key worked and I crept on in. The odour inside was sickening and the sight of the place wasn't any better on my stomach. Everywhere was tinged with black and there were puddles from the water hoses. It didn't look like anything much could be salvaged. There isn't much of a worse sight for a music fan than records and guitars all mangled and melted into each other. Especially as they were mine. And my livelihood.

"Hello?" called David.

I heard his feet tread noisily over the hallway scattered with various charred remains.

"In here," I called.

"Jesus, it really is bad," he confirmed, coming in and standing beside me.

"Yep, don't think we'll be open for a few days," I said with a wry laugh.

I searched his face. Then dropped my tone.

"Thanks for coming, sorry I can't offer you anything."

"No, that's all right."

"Well, that's probably not quite true. I can offer you one thing. I can offer you the chance to tell the truth."

His forehead creased and he moved awkwardly to one side. I felt my phone buzz in my pocket. Now wasn't the time for somebody to offer me a new broadband deal.

"What are you talking about?"

"Like how you were behind tip offs about Ricky Randall."

His face crinkled into an awkward smile, "What are you talking about?"

"Or that there was no plan to get the band going again. Because you hadn't even seen Alan in years. But mostly you should tell the truth about your sister."

The last part dug home. There was anguish on his face. And something else? What was it- guilt?

"Why are you trying to trace Randall?" I asked more to myself than to him.

"Do you want to kill him? Is that why you were covering your tracks and asked me not to mention your name?"

Now any hope of keeping his secret hidden had been washed away, along with the sweat dripping off his long nose.

"I…" He started, and shook his head, looking towards the ground. His eyes welled and he stifled a sob.

"Fuck me," I said quietly, the truth finally dawning on me, "You didn't want anyone to find him did you? You made that shit up to put people off the track."

His body seemed to crumble further. Every word chipped another part of him away.

My stupid phone continued to buzz away in my pocket.

"Because nobody would find him, would they?" I licked my lips, "Forty years ago. You had already killed him."

He couldn't hold it in any longer. Any of it. He broke down.

"I was angry... I didn't mean to..." he said in between sobs, "He fucking raped her! Just fifteen, fifteen..." he cried, shaking his head.

I took a deep breath, making up my mind.

"I was on my way to meet Ricky one time," he continued, sniffing, "When I got there..."

I raised my hand, "Don't tell me anymore. I don't need to know. I'm not gonna tell anyone."

And with that I ushered him from my burnt out shop and that's the last I ever saw him.

Chapter 18

After I had locked up (for whatever point there was in that) I walked slowly back towards my car. I felt the vibrating more keenly and realised my phone had been ringing on and off the whole time. I pulled it out.

Fifteen missed calls from Pav.

Something's wrong.

I quickly pressed to call back and waited anxiously for her to pick up. I had a bad feeling.

I could hear my own deep breathing echoing in my ear, then it was coupled with Pav's, then joined by her shaky scream.

"Jimmy! Jimmy where have you been?" she shouted, in amongst violent crying.

"What happened? What is it love?"

My voice sounded like a little boy's.

"They stuck a petrol bomb through our door Jimmy. Through our letterbox." She stopped, racked by crying.

"What? Are you okay? Is Skye okay? Jesus Pav."

"We're okay."

One channel of relief flooded through me. The other channel remained blocked. It felt like my arteries were blocked too, I was sure I going to have a heart attack.

"Did it not go off?"

"It wasn't lit," she said before one giant sob emerged from deep inside her, "Thank God Jimmy... thank God... Skye picked it up... and carried it into me."

"Christ. Oh love, I'm so sorry. I'll be right there. I'll get home to you now. Don't speak to anyone else."

"Not to the police?"

"No, not yet. Lock the doors, I'm coming."

"Hurry Jimmy."

As I sped along the thirty limit roads closer to sixty I knew I wasn't going straight home. I wasn't in control, not the human side anyway. I felt all animal.

I had been to his house once before, a long time ago, when my brother had been one of the top dogs. Now things had changed. Everything had changed. The fury I felt was like nothing I had ever experienced. I could have broken down stone walls with my bare fists. My daughter had picked up a fucking petrol bomb. Rage pulsed from every inch of my being.

...

It's all a blur, but I do remember running up the path to the semi in the estate in Dundonald. I hammered on the door. I didn't give the guy answering any time. I smashed the door into his face and the bone in his nose made a sickening crack. He dropped a gun to the floor as blood shot out from his face. I stepped inside and shut the door behind me. I uppercut him as he bent stooped from the initial blow. He hit the dirt, most likely already unconscious. I skipped around him and into the living room, my arms loose at my sides. At the far end of the room was a nervous looking Michael Kinney, moving round a table. He was slowly approaching me, with a little flick knife in one hand.

Every part of me tingled with a jagged anticipation.

"Have you never seen Crocodile fucking Dundee?"

I reached into my pocket and pulled out the kitchen knife that had been there since England, "That's not a knife, this is a fucking knife."

For a top guy, who'd seen a few things, he looked petrified. I must have looked liked I meant business. He threw the knife down beside him and raised his hands,

"Okay Jimmy, let's talk about this thing."

I threw my own knife down and pushed him onto the sofa. He was weak as a kitten. Or it felt that way. I climbed above him and began raining punches into his face. It felt good.

Really good.

It felt like honest, satisfying work. Once he gave up struggling and my fists began to hurt, I climbed off of him. He turned to the side, hacking, gargling blood. He threw up over the sofa, then coughed some more. His face was a bloodied mess.

"You stay the fuck away from my family," I growled and left.

Chapter 19

We held each other for a long time.

The three of us.

Clinging to each other on the bed. We hadn't talked much, just a little. This was what we needed. Pav knew most of what she needed to know from my swollen, blood stained knuckles.

Skye was almost asleep on my shoulder and I gently pushed Pav's head away, so I could look at her properly.

"I'm so sorry love."

"You don't need to be Jimmy," she whispered, touching my cheek.

"I should have been here."

"You couldn't know."

"I think we should go away," I said suddenly.

She looked quizzically at me, "Really? What… you mean that?"

"Yeah, why not? Let's get away from all of this shit."

Her eyes appeared less clouded. Maybe it was the arrival of hope.

"I think I would like that Jimmy. We could start again."

She held Skye's tiny hand inside her own.

"Let's do it then."

"Where would we go?"

"How about Lanzarote?"

...

Excerpt from The Belfast News column: 'Natalie's Noise'

"The *noise* from this week included something rather unpleasant, readers. It reminded us that there are those in our society who still hark back to the bad old days. Those bent on those old ways of the paramilitary and the bomb. But there was also a piece of good news to this story. One man was on the receiving end of such a people- he was attacked, had his shop burned down and his family threatened. He stood up to the bully and literally slapped him down. I can't give any names for legal reasons right now, but watch this space for the whole story. I don't intend to be cryptic here readers. In the meantime, well played Jimmy."

...

Discover more of the author's work here-

https://amzn.to/2F9J2ui

Social media-

https://facebook.com/simonmaltmancrimefiction

https://twitter.com/simonmaltman

https://simonmaltmanblogs.blogspot.com

Printed in Great Britain
by Amazon